SACRED

PRESENCE

In Search of
the New Story

Robert C. Wild

Note for Librarians: a cataloguing record for this book that includes Dewey Classification and US Library of Congress numbers is available from the National Library of Canada. The complete cataloguing record can be obtained from the National Library's online database at: www.nlc-bnc.ca/amicus/index-e.html
ISBN 1-4120-3118-4

TRAFFORD

This book was published on-demand in cooperation with Trafford Publishing.
On-demand publishing is a unique process and service of making a book available for retail sale to the public taking advantage of on-demand manufacturing and Internet marketing. On-demand publishing includes promotions, retail sales, manufacturing, order fulfilment, accounting and collecting royalties on behalf of the author.

Suite 6E, 2333 Government St., Victoria, B.C. V8T 4P4, CANADA
Phone   250-383-6864   Toll-free 1-888-232-4444 (Canada & US)
Fax   250-383-6804   E-mail   sales@trafford.com
Web site www.trafford.com   TRAFFORD PUBLISHING IS A DIVISION OF TRAFFORD HOLDINGS LTD.
Trafford Catalogue #04-0945   www.trafford.com/robots/04-0945.html
10   9   8   7   6   5   4   3

For peoples, generally, their story of the universe and the human role in the universe is their primary source of intelligibility and value. . . . The deepest crises experienced by any society are those moments of change when the story becomes inadequate for meeting the survival demands of a present situation.

Thomas Berry
"The Dream of the Earth"

We can now put Darwin together with Einstein and Hubble. When the Christian creed fails to connect with these scales of time, it loses its link to the galaxies or its necessary ingredient of wildness; it begins to feel conventional, domesticated, tamed, and without power. Something essential has been lost. The juice has gone out of it.

David Toolan
"At Home in the Cosmos"

PREFACE

One blistering hot, mid summer Saturday in the early 1960s, a young clergyman made his way by train from Saskatoon to Unity, in the province of Saskatchewan. His destination was the four-point parish of Macklin where he would conduct Sunday services because the local incumbent was on holiday. The train journey was a 'milk run', with lengthy stops at each small town. He could see the dry prairie alive with grasshoppers, a sure sign that the summer sun's heat had settled into the land.

At Unity he was met by a farmer, a few years his senior in age, who was to take him from the Unity train station to the town of Macklin, about an hour's drive. As the two men were strangers, the conversation was rather slow and a little awkward. Dust from the gravel highway rose in thick clouds behind the car, aggravating the uncomfortable heat of the day. The cleric licked his dry lips and asked his companion, "Doesn't the hotel in Macklin have a beverage room?" The driver stole a quizzical glance at the man beside him, clad from head to toe in black clerical attire with a gleaming white collar at his neck. Cautiously, he replied, "Well, yes, I guess so." "Would you mind if we stopped there for a drink, before you drop me at the home where I am to have dinner and stay the night?" Another glance sideways, and the driver agreed this would be possible.

At the hotel, he led the cleric into the beverage room. The man appeared somewhat embarrassed to be seen in the company of his unusual charge as he was now in the presence of a goodly number of local farmers well known to himself. The two new arrivals sat at a table together, ordered their beer, and continued their previous somewhat laboured conversation.

Very soon one of the other farmers drew his chair to their table and asked if they minded if he put a question to "the reverend". Permission given, the conversation quickly became animated. Other men now brought over their own chairs, and then more tables were brought to enlarge the circle of convivial drinking and conversation. When an hour or so later it was time to disperse to their homes for dinner, some twenty men terminated a conversation which had canvassed religious concerns they had been wondering about for years. None of them had indicated he belonged to a church. And, as I remember, few of them were present at the town or country churches where I presided the next day.

For nearly half a century I have been present at similar discussions in living rooms, church halls, conference centres, university gatherings, and public meetings - but in only a few beverage rooms. Each time I have realized that contemporary church teaching is failing to engage the urgent religious questions of ordinary people. Has this problem resulted chiefly from unfamiliar religious vocabulary, from theological language and concepts which are out of touch with daily life? Or does it come from a larger problem where a traditional Christian world view no longer speaks to a majority of people? Is it because the Bible is a closed book to the vast majority of people? Or does the problem of discontinuity between church and world have deeper and more complex roots? These are the questions which drive this book.

My findings have been greatly influenced by two factors which I believe are at the root of this discontinuity. Both of them come from the pre-eminent place which the scientific method occupies in the modern world. First, the physical sciences - especially biology, geology and astronomy - have revolutionized our perception of the cosmos. We now have a view of human life which must take into account the enormous and expanding macro universe which originated some fourteen or fifteen billion years ago and in which our Earth is a tiny speck. We are aware also that a micro universe exists as the underlying reality of Earth and all its creatures. There is a physical reality of quantum motion and matter which is fundamental to everything we are and do.

The second major factor which has distanced the modern mind and spirit from classical Christian teaching is the work of the social sciences. In particular, history, sociology, psychology and archaeology have revolutionized our understanding of the forces affecting personal and

i

social development. We are learning to think contextually: everything on Earth is inter-connected. Incessant interactions, especially among humans and between humans and our physical environment, profoundly affect our personal and social lives. It is said that "we are what we eat", but just as truly, who we are is an expression of being in relationship to everything and everyone in our world. To experience this brings a revolution in consciousness.

Even though relatively few of us have detailed knowledge of research in the physical and social sciences, all of us are caught up in a culture which is heavily influenced by the scientific method. Our consciousness is very different from that of the people of the Bible or of the early Jesus Movement. The literature and the traditions which they developed were circumscribed by a relatively small world view. They lived on flat Earth, viewed as the centre of the universe, under heaven, with eternity beyond time and space. Their understanding of social dynamics, of the forces which influence human life, was very limited. They believed that the gods daily influenced the course of their personal lives and of their societies. The contemporary world view which we take for granted was totally beyond their imagination.

The radical disconnection of an increasing number of modern people of Western religious and cultural background from the received faith traditions of Christianity can be traced to this difference between two world views. It seems apparent to me that this is a process which cannot be reversed. If there are to be vital and creative Christian communities present within coming generations, they will be grounded in a careful re-examination and renewal of our traditions, including an appreciation of the Bible different from that which most of us have received.

The work of re-examination and renewal is already underway. Scholars of religion and of the Bible have been giving the ordinary enquirer solid ground on which to rethink and redesign his or her own faith journey.

This book is written as a contribution to that process for people who come from Christian religious training or are new enquirers. Throughout my adult life I have been a student and a practitioner of Christian faith, constantly discovering that I am being challenged to rethink and redesign my pilgrimage. During my lifetime there has been a veritable avalanche of new thought and practice from which I continue to benefit. It is my hope that other pilgrims will benefit from the fruits of my journey as I share them in this book.

Throughout the years of reflection, and of trial and error, I have been nurtured and guided by the works of scholars in several disciplines. From them I have received an exciting wealth of new insights and to them I owe an enormous debt of gratitude. In recent years I have encountered research and writing dealing with 'the new cosmology'. This work has given me a new context within which to place everything I have thought and done over the years. And in addition to these intellectual mentors, I have a great many friends to thank for uncounted hours of conversation and disputation. I extend special gratitude to Audrey Wild, Clare and Don Vipond, Pat Cherewick, Ann Anchor and Margaret Cameron for their continuing encouragement and support, to Margaret for designing the cover for this book, to Andrea Rankin for her expert editing of the original manuscript, and to Nicki Cameron for her careful and precise preparation of the finished work.

D.T. Niles, a famous Christian teacher from India, once said that "evangelism is one beggar showing another beggar where to find food." I have been blessed with innumerable people who have shown me where to find food, and I hope in this book to point to some of the sources which I have found to be the most inspiring, the most life-giving.

Robert C. Wild
Salt Spring Island, B.C.
V8K 1B6
<wildacre@saltspring.com>
2004.

This revised edition of SACRED PRESENCE includes minor corrections to the text and clarification of several passages.

Salt Spring Island, 2005

CONTENTS

Quotations from the Bible
are from the New Revised Standard Version
Oxford University Press, 1991

INTRODUCTION

> Everyone who has a common desire to observe the
> Christian worship may now freely and unconditionally
> endeavour to do so without let or hindrance.
>> Constantine, "Act of Toleration"

In the year 313 of the Common Era, the Roman Emperor Constantine recognized Christianity as the official religion of his domains. Leading up to this event, a gradual and somewhat underground process of conceiving, elaborating and consolidating the church's faith and worship had taken place. But now, with the emperor's sanction, an emerging Christian orthodoxy was free to become a unified and officially recognized system of belief and religious practice. Henceforth, deviations from the norm would be suppressed as heresy. The religious culture known as Christendom began to take definite shape, and by the year 800 had secured hegemony throughout much of Eurasia. During ensuing centuries its indelible mark extended everywhere on that continent and into lands colonized by Europeans. A way of faith and life became established and it endured more or less intact for more than a thousand years.

This has now changed irrevocably. Many, perhaps most, contemporary Western people experience orthodox Christian faith and liturgy as being at least problematic and possibly obsolete. This book is written in response to this development and seeks to engage with the many creative responses which are contributing to a new statement of the traditional faith story.

In Chapter One I review briefly some of the main issues under discussion. Also included is a brief introduction to the 'new cosmology' as a necessary context for any attempted restatement of Christian belief and practice.

Chapter Two introduces Israel's national 'myth', a Grand Narrative which tells of the heroic age of that nation. Within this national story particular attention is paid to two elements. First we notice a radical social vision which was legislated within the Mosaic covenant. Second we trace the evolution of Israel's image of God, developing from a warrior image early in its history to the image of the compassionate God of prophet and psalmist.

Chapter Three is a reconstruction of the meaning of Jesus of Nazareth's life and work, making extensive use of contemporary biblical scholarship.

Chapter Four suggests that a pursuit of power by the Christian church throughout its history is rooted in the classical Christian Doctrine of the Atonement. This teaching affirms that Jesus of Nazareth's death on a cross brought to humanity the possibility of salvation from eternal death, a fate which came upon us as the bitter fruit of sin. This chapter provides a careful and critical consideration of the doctrine and suggests reasons why it must be abandoned.

Chapter Five returns to the theme of the new cosmology. The old, traditional cosmology provided a basis for classical Christian thought. However, as that cosmology is seen now to be obsolete, traditional Christianity is found wanting. I propose ways in which insights of the new cosmology might creatively engage with biblical religion.

Chapter Six calls our attention to Earth as the originating source of and continuing support for human life, the supreme sign for us of the divine generosity. I discuss the appropriate response for us to make to that generosity. I also note how radical injustices in society mock the true meaning of the divine generosity.

Chapter Seven considers many ways in which the implications of the issues raised in this book impact Christian faith and life as they are expressed in our liturgical gatherings and personal devotions.

To assist readers I have supplied summaries at the end of each chapter.

A SHORT GLOSSARY

There are overlapping meanings among a few of the terms frequently used in this book. The terms elude exact definition because they seek to point to Ultimate Reality which is beyond our ability to describe and can only be named through symbolic words and deeds. I see these terms as holding a 'continuum of meaning', moving from the most familiar to the most sublime.

GOD . . . is the word most often used by us to name Ultimate Reality as we encounter it.   But the word is used among us so lightly, casually and frequently that it is often difficult to know what meaning is intended. Sometimes the word carries heavy anthropomorphic overtones, which risks idolatry and false familiarity.   On the other hand, I recognize that the word 'God' can carry a strong sense of spiritual communion with the universal Other.   The word 'God' can signify our sense of a divine Companion who walks the dusty way of life's journey with us. I tend to use this word when none of the others below fits comfortably into what I am writing.

THE DIVINE . . . is a name I use to point to our experience of a cosmic reality, conceived by human imagination and reason to be the indwelling force, power or energy which sustains the universe. Our experience of this reality can be so vivid that people speak of themselves as being in the presence of the Divine. We say then that this relationship is 'personal' - but this does not mean that the Divine is a person reduceable to human categories. Symbolism of all kinds has been used to represent the Divine in social life and in personal thoughts and feelings.

THE HOLY ONE . . . pertains to the Divine as being morally and spiritually pure. Holiness is an attribute of the Divine, but can also stand for the Divine when that attribute is being accented. Thus, I speak of 'the Holy One' when referring primarily to the sublime righteousness of the Divine. But holiness is also a general category and can be used to refer to any person or thing which we regard as approaching moral and spiritual purity.

THE SACRED . . . points to depths of the Divine beyond all human experience. That aspect of the Sacred which presents Itself to us as personal I name 'the Divine'. Sacred is the more diffuse term, Divine is the more specific term; and both refer to the same Reality. The Sacred and the Divine form a continuum, with the former signifying Ultimate Reality as remote, mysterious, ubiquitous, and the latter signifying Ultimate Reality as intimate, particular, specific, personalized.

MYSTERY . . . signifies a postulate of faith. It is Ultimate Reality which lies beyond everything our faculties - spiritual, mental and physical - can access. Perhaps it is a way of saying that there is a limit to what we can experience, intuit, imagine, reason - that the full range of our human perceptions does not and cannot exhaust Reality. Mystery is opaque, obscure, postulated; but the Sacred shines, blinds, amazes, brings wonder.

1

A TIME OF TRANSITION

> A pitiless civil war has broken out in the vitals of our age . .
> . . between the old, formerly omnipotent myth which has
> vented its strength, yet which fights desparately to
> regulate our lives a while longer, and the new myth which
> is battling, still awkwardly and without organization, to
> govern our souls.
>
> Nikos Kazantzakis, "Report to Greco"

MYTH TO SUSTAIN A FABRIC OF MEANINGS

Human beings cannot exist without carefully conceived webs of meaning by which to articulate who they are and how they shall live as part of the universe. These webs of meaning have usually been expressed in communal storytelling, the most famous of which give us the great mythological traditions of humanity. Cultures, both pre-literate and literate, provide us with interlocking stories which describe how different peoples understood their respective origins and how their common life was guided and sustained. Our own western society is no exception to this general rule; we too have our constitutive myths.

A particularly vivid account of the kind of function served by communal myth is provided by Mircea Eliade ("The Sacred and The Profane", 33):

> According to the traditions of an Arunta tribe [Australian nomads], the Achilpa, in mythical times the divine being Numbakula cosmicized their future territory . . . . From the trunk of a gum tree Numbakula fashioned the sacred pole and, after anointing it with blood, climbed it and disappeared into the sky. This pole represents a cosmic axis, for it is around the sacred pole that territory becomes habitable, hence is transformed into a world. The sacred pole consequently plays an important role ritually. During their wanderings the Achilpa always carry it with them and choose the directions they are to take by the direction toward which it bends. . . .
>
> For the pole to be broken denotes catastrophe; it is like "the end of the world," reversion to chaos. Spencer and Gillen report that once, when the pole was

broken, the entire clan were in consternation; they wandered about aimlessly for a time, and finally lay down on the ground together and waited for death to overtake them.

All stable human groups live within certain shared social, economic and religious assumptions which govern their lives. Each group accepts its own social patterns and sacred myths as normative, as providing the vital expression of its 'fabric of meanings'. This last phrase comes from a seminal book by Peter Berger and Thomas Luckmann, "The Social Construction of Reality":

> Only a very limited group of people in any society engages in theorizing, in the business of "ideas" . . . But everyone in society participates in its "knowledge" in one way or another. Put differently, only a few are concerned with the theoretical interpretation of the world, but everyone lives in a world of some sort. . . .It is precisely this "knowledge" that constitutes the fabric of meanings without which no society could exist. (p.15)

Berger and Luckmann demonstrate that the mental and spiritual world in which we live - the fabric of meanings and values which control how we feel, think and behave - is a social construction. We create this encompassing reality, this "lived world", as we develop the many aspects of common life: technology, methods of commerce, agricultural practices, legal structures, economic theory, artistic norms, recreational activities, patterns of dress, culinary preferences, social mores, religious beliefs and rituals, etc. Vital values and meanings are generated within all this activity and, like the many threads of a piece of cloth, they become woven together into a comprehensive social fabric - even though the whole is never self-consistent.

The fabric of meanings in a given culture guides and supports the people of that culture in the face of the imponderable mysteries in which human life is embedded. This socialized intellectual fabric is the work of creative human imagination, and it is sustained by mythic themes and stories.

Any given fabric of meanings endures as a working mythology only so long as those who believe in it consider it to be consistent with human experience and reasoning. Myths must 'make sense' in their own time and place. But our experience changes over time, and human reasoning powers are constantly developing. Reason probes and experience challenges and eventually demystifies what has hitherto been felt to be enduring sacred tradition; it undermines the power of that mythology. Professor Paul Tillich said that a myth which has lost its power to control human behaviour has become a 'broken' myth. The biblical story of Adam and Eve is an example of a myth which formerly held enormous power but which today is broken.

The fabric of meanings intrinsic to any society is internalized so deeply that most people live their personal and social existence without giving deliberate or conscious attention to these meanings. And for the most part they anticipate that this more or less seamless fabric of meanings will continue indefinitely into the future.

Customs, beliefs and patterns of a given social group are more lived than discussed, more practised than debated by its members. Nevertheless, in each society there are ideologues (priests, philosophers, chiefs, shamans, political leaders, media commentators, writers, poets, et al.) who in service of the common good seek to articulate and stress the importance and validity of existing patterns. These advocates more or less understand the central cultural and creedal affirmations, accept and endorse them, and in various ways seek to make secure the social norms which they support. However, no patterns of economic, social and religious life are eternal. Many forces, internal and external, work to alter them - forces more extensive and subtle than the breaking of a sacred pole, and seldom with the same immediate and drastic consequences.

As a child growing up in the city of Montreal during the 1930's and 40's, I frequently visited nearby rural areas of the province of Québec. In each of the small towns a prominent Roman Catholic church building stood at the centre, a pivotal religious institution that engendered a network of customs which were taken for granted. During three centuries of teaching and preaching, the church sought to help its people adopt the creative values which Roman Catholic religion brought to their lives. For several decades leading up to the 1960's, however, Québec was moving toward an economic, social and religious upheaval known as the "Quiet Revolution". And in the '60s a significant section of the population of the province shook off the iron grip of church rule and began a new era.

This raises some interesting questions. Did that social revolution occur because twentieth century Québequois had failed to grasp the true value of their inherited religious culture? Had the teachings of the church been too little seen and understood, too poorly taught and too little believed? Or had the tides of time and the forces of modernity convinced an important segment of the population that traditional patterns of both religious faith and social practice had become inadequate for the future? As it has turned out, the particular religious teaching and practice long prevalent in Québec is no longer able to inspire the belief and behaviour it once clearly identified and strongly advocated. New values are being espoused, new ways of living being tested, and fledgling convictions and commitments are struggling to win hearts and minds in order to build a different future.

THE CHRIST MYTH

The recent history of the province of Québec reveals what has been taking place slowly for a much longer time throughout Christendom. For more than fifteen hundred years after the time of Jesus of Nazareth, the Christian church put in place what can be called the "Christ Myth". (The term 'myth' signifies creative and dynamic ideological forces which sustain a fabric of meanings.) The Christian church fashioned a large, credible picture of reality within which people could feel secure and by this myth our forebears received spiritual vision and values to govern their lives. This particular fabric of meanings took definite shape in late Roman and early medieval times and lasted without serious challenge until the Enlightenment of the 18th century. The traditional Christ Myth consists of several key elements which may be summarized as follows.

The boundaries of the drama are Heaven and Hell. Existing between these metaphysical realities is Earth created by a God whose dwelling place is in Heaven. Human life began on this earth in a state of innocence, but human beings 'fell' from God's favour by disobedience, and so God acted through his divine Son Jesus to bring them back to himself (in this fabric of meanings God is unequivocally male). This was achieved because Jesus gave up his life for us. There will be a Day of Judgment in which God will hold human beings accountable for all they have done, and the creation will reach its appointed fulfilment. The kind of life we live on earth determines whether or not Jesus' sacrifice will save us for eternal life with God.

This sweeping fabric of meanings for human life is properly termed 'mythical'. Though key elements in the story are represented as historical, they are actually metaphysical (beyond physical description and measurement): a flat Earth at the centre of the cosmos with Heaven above and Hell beneath, an originating time of perfect beauty and bliss, a first man and woman committing sin against God which stains every human, salvation of humanity from eternal loss by one human/Divine death - these and other metaphysical features of the Story captured human imagination and shaped human behaviour. The Christ Myth offered a mental and spiritual world within which the people of Christendom could interpret, and participate in, the human drama from its beginnings in time to its fulfilment in the eternal realms.

The Christian church gave humanity the sublime Christ Myth. The church was also the guarantor of the truth of the myth, and for about 1500 years both church and myth exercised extensive control over how Europeans and their converts overseas felt about themselves and about the world in which they lived. A central limitation inherent in every myth, however, is that it has power to convince and control only so long as there is no obvious credibility gap between its picture of reality and what is securely known by observation and experience. Eventually every myth becomes eroded by advances in human knowledge of the natural world.

The first decisive erosion of the mythological drama of Christian belief was the declaration by Copernicus that our planet is round and is not the centre of anything. Other scientists and philosophers such as Galileo and Isaac Newton expanded the new learning.

> Newton had provided a blueprint for the workings of the universe which seemed as reliable and predictable as a mechanical clock, and in so doing he realized the worst nightmares of the medieval Church . . . God's

9

intervention in this new materialist universe was limited to providing the initial wind-up to get it all going, and the important consequence of that was that it could then carry on running without benefit of clergy.

(W. Rowland, "Ockham's Razor", 163)

Key elements of the myth were threatened.

A second blow was the increasing appeal to, and use of, inductive reasoning, in contrast to the church's standard theological method of deductive reasoning. The deductive method begins with established premises (in religion these are usually called 'revealed truth') and uses logical reasoning to reach conclusions. Inductive reasoning, on the other hand (often called the 'scientific method'), works with observable data which can be obtained by standard, repeatable procedures and tested for consistent conclusions. During the last three or four centuries, the results of inductive reasoning have challenged the sovereign rule of established authority, especially of theology which had been termed the 'Queen of the Sciences'. As a result, the dogmas of the church have not been secure from critical scrutiny and rejection.

A third blow to the Christ Myth was geological evidence indicating a much older Earth than had previously been affirmed. Moreover, it seems that all life is a chain, a biological evolution from elementary chemical origins to the most complex organisms. There is no discernible time of a human 'fall from innocence' and no obvious eternal purpose in this evolutionary process.

Further undermining of the Christ Myth came from depth psychology. Human consciousness is pictured as a tiny protrusion riding on a massive unconscious psyche. The realm of the unconscious provides us with creative powers, dreams, fantasies, slips of the tongue, unexpected memories - it is a vast storehouse of psychic energy and experience. When it is realized that much of our behaviour comes from these mysterious subterranean psychic depths, what can be meant by personal responsibility? What can be meant by sin, guilt before God, and divine forgiveness?

In these and other developments the Bible itself was not left unscathed. Scholarship made it clear that biblical writings have a long and complex history of formation, transmission, editing and writing. The origin of the biblical documents is more human and less divine than had been supposed. Moreover, their correct interpretation requires an educated understanding of the cultural contexts within which they emerged.

Thus, several centuries of battering has left the inherited Christian world view without persuasive power for many people of traditional Christian cultures. And this has created a serious deficit in our mental and spiritual universe. We no longer have a large, credible picture, a commonly-accepted fabric of meanings in which to place ourselves and to feel at home, in which we are secure and able to act with purpose. Though many persons of Christian origin can point to distinctive elements in the Christian story which for them retain worth (such as Christian morality), a total pattern of meaning is missing.

OLD-TIME RELIGION IN DECLINE

In this manner, long established patterns of belief have been strained to the breaking point and Western society is becoming less functional, less stable. (It should be said that the contemporary social malaise is the result of more than the demise of the Christ Myth, though its loss has removed the fundamental Story by which our culture formerly lived.) In response to this creeping loss of social and personal meaning, efforts have been made to deny and delay the spreading religious decay. Voices are heard offering new versions of the original Myth, sketching variations in traditional belief patterns which might light a way forward. New Age mythologies are persuading some people to forsake Christianity for their alternative visions of reality. And there is conflict between what has been valued in the past and what is being proposed for the future.

Signs of this tension are evident in many segments of our society. Family life in Western culture, for example, had a normative pattern for many centuries, a pattern which accorded with pre-eminent church teaching. But in recent decades, experiments have been and are being made in diverse forms of family, redesigning the basic kin group. This phenomenon has caused great stress among us, and defenders of the old teaching are often in conflict with proponents of more recent expressions of family.

11

In a similar manner, we have experienced the gradual eclipse of some long-standing imperatives of the traditional Christ Myth. Religious traditions which used to shape personal and community life are disintegrating. Worship at church each Sunday, daily prayer, regular Bible reading at home, commitment to biblical moral values - these and other religious practices have been in decline in the West for more than a century. Growing numbers of people no longer consider the old-time religion adequate to shape our fundamental feelings about the present or to guide our deliberations and actions for future life on this planet. Richard R. Friedman, in "The Hidden Book of the Bible" (55), makes this observation:

> Our time might more properly be described as *beneath* good and evil. If this were just an intellectual game that we played in school and college, it would be one thing. But it is not harmless. In our confused century, we have seen suffering beyond counting, comparing, or describing.

Within the churches there is considerable resistance by some members to efforts made by other members who want to reshape and renew biblical faith in response to the changes mentioned above. Some of this resistance is an understandable reluctance for radical change. Old-time religion is thought by many people to be the one thing which does not change. After all, isn't it here that we find the Rock of Ages? There is a very natural feeling among deeply religious people that there can be nothing ahead which will be as serviceable as that which is slipping away. They have a conviction that the old served us well and that it can continue to do so. They ask: what assurance could anyone possibly have that, if we release our hold on the familiar anchor, we will not be shipwrecked?

We are witnessing - and it should surprise no one - strong efforts to keep our society rooted in traditional religion. Assisting this is the force of inertia in a large segment of society, people who would rather just get on with life with a minimum of intellectual and spiritual endeavour. They make small adjustments here and there, both in how they live and in what they believe, so as to accomodate the pressure of whatever seems

12

inevitable. But they express no interest in the renewal of Christian thought or practice.

In response to legitimate anxieties and concerns, however, it must be urged that we have experienced at least a century of decline in the ability of inherited forms of religious teaching and practice to win human minds and hearts. Western society has become spiritually adrift and morally bankrupt. And so I want to ask conservative believers: in view of the long history of our tradition, can we not trust the God of biblical faith to lead us to insights for new times, to wisdom born of the information and skills which have been accumulating rapidly in recent decades? Surely we can expect that the wisdom of past and present together can speak with vitality to the unfamiliar landscape which lies ahead.

Within all the confusion of cultural and religious change there are indeed signs that we are being led into new paths of faith, including fundamental changes in our image of God. As we learn to use the creative skills and insights being fashioned within our secularized culture, we can re-encounter our tradition with excitement and expectation. A revised myth, a new Story, will emerge: "Symbol and myth are forms of the human consciousness which are always present. One can replace one myth by another, but one cannot remove the myth from man's(sic) spiritual life." (Paul Tillich, "Dynamics of Faith", 50) This is a basic conviction driving the writing of this book.

Many Christians today understand that we read our sacred texts and respond to the life, death and resurrection of Jesus of Nazareth within cultural contexts very different from those which gave form to the classical Christian world view. The people who wrote the Bible could not realize that their words would one day be read in a world so radically different from their own that what they wrote would fail to communicate readily what they meant. The Bible's meanings cannot be understood by us without careful reflection on the ways in which the cultures of those times influenced how biblical people developed their story of Reality. At the best of times, human communication is always difficult; when attempting to bridge many centuries and to overcome deep cultural chasms, those difficulties are compounded. I am grateful that biblical scholars are constantly assisting us in the work of interpretation.

We are people of a humanist, rationalist, scientific and technological culture. We have profound and difficult questions to which traditional Christian teaching is unable to make adequate response. On the other hand, our religious tradition has rich resources in intellectual, moral and mystical experience and insight to bring to our search for vital religious belief and practice. And we should be greatly encouraged by knowing that scientists have developed an illuminating story about the cosmos and its fifteen billion year evolution which will enrich our religious reflection.

EMERGENCE OF THE NEW STORY

In the last two centuries, scientific investigation has been accumulating large amounts of data from which some contemporary philosophers of science have generated a new story of the cosmos. The data describe the evolution, structure and motion of matter/energy in the universe, from the microcosmic to the macrocosmic. The new cosmology does not apply only to one society, culture or religion; it is the common property of all humanity because it tells the one story to which we can all subscribe. Thomas Berry offers us this summary of the work of countless scientists:

> The story of the universe is the story of the emergence of a galactic system in which each new level of expression emerges through the urgency of self-transcendence. Hydrogen in the presence of some millions of degrees of heat emerges into helium. After the stars take shape as oceans of fire in the heavens, they go though a sequence of transformations. Some eventually explode into the stardust out of which the solar system and the earth take shape. Earth gives unique expression of itself in its rock and crystalline structures and in the variety of living forms, until humans appear as the moment in which the unfolding universe becomes conscious of itself. . . . We bear the universe in our being as the universe bears us in its being. The two have a total presence to each other and to that deeper mystery out of which both the universe and ourselves have emerged.
>
> ("The Dream of the Earth", 132)

That deeper mystery, the Divine, Sacred Presence, has been the subject of human myth-making since the dawn of the human race. Through these myths humanity has provided itself with a succession of socially created fabrics of meaning within which to live and work out the significance of human existence as a wondrous gift of the Sacred. Thomas Berry proposes that human myth-making can be seen in three historic ages, the first of which predates our historical memory:

> The human sense of an all-pervasive, numinous, or sacred power gave to life a deep security. It enabled us over a long period of time to establish ourselves within a realm of consciousness of high spiritual, social, and artistic development. This was the period when the divinities were born in human consciousness as expressions of those profound spiritual orientations that emerged from the earth process into our unconscious depth, then as symbols into our conscious mind, and finally into visible expression.
>
> (*ibid*, 39)

A well known example of this process in the Western world are the myths and legends of ancient Greece, which populated existence with the Olympian gods.

According to Berry, this early expression of spiritual awareness, of spiritual energy, was followed by the age of the classical cultures. This age gave to humanity the great world religions that are still with us: Hinduism, Buddhism, Judaism, Islam and Christianity. But the last four or five thousand years were not merely a specific historical period of new learning and technical advances; they held "a kind of energy pulsating in and through sacred liturgies carried out in seasonal life periods, as well as in the personal life cycle from birth to maturity to death." (*ibid*, 27) That is: the spiritual energy found in pre-historic humanity was succeeded by a new spiritual energy of the great world religions.

About four centuries ago, a third human epoch began to assert itself in the rise of a scientific and technological culture in Europe. The new industrial age overlapped the legacy of the classical cultures and challenged their myths. In the West, this brought about the decline of the Christ Myth. In addition, Berry points out, the new fabric of meanings created by scientific investigation and achievement "was less concerned with [the earth's natural rhythms] than with physical forces at work in the

15

universe and the manner in which we could avail ourselves of these energies to serve our own well-being. . . . The experience [in the West] of sacred communion with the earth disappeared." (*ibid*, 40-41)

As part of its pragmatic approach to life, the developing scientific and technological age generated its own mystique and promoted its own myth, the 'myth of progress'. This myth contains a drive toward:

> a millenium of earthly beatitude. . . . Human effort, not divine grace, was the instrument for this paradisal realization. The scientists and inventors, the bankers and commercial magnates, were now the saints who would reign. . . . It was an energy revolution not only in terms of the physical energies now available to us, but also in terms of the psychic energies . . . [by which we sought] to attain such power as was formerly attributed only to the natural or to the divine.
>
> (*ibid*, 40)

For more than a century the myth of progress has captivated the minds and hearts of most westernized people. It has shaped the most powerful fabric of meanings of our time and has been the source of the spiritual energy of industrial society. The myth has justified itself through the achievement of previously undreamt uses for the resources of Earth. Tragically, however, a different and dark legacy of this myth is present in extensive species extermination, massive pollution, colossal problems of waste disposal and increasing numbers of people existing in endemic poverty. The industrial mythic energy has spread itself into every corner of the Earth and is leaving its harmful mark on every process of the biosphere. Berry comments:

> The remedy for this is to establish a deeper understanding of the spiritual dynamics of the universe as revealed through our own empirical insight into the mysteries of its functioning. In this late twentieth century that can be done with a clarity never before available to us. Empirical inquiry into the universe reveals that from its beginning in the galactic system to its earthly expression in human consciousness the universe carries within itself a psychic-spiritual as well as a physical-material dimension. Otherwise human consciousness emerges out of nowhere.
>
> (*ibid*, 131)

Human consciousness is singled out by the new cosmology as the psychic-spiritual energy which holds the promise of the future. And so Berry concludes his historical survey with this claim:

> Presently we are entering another historical period, one that might be designated as the ecological age. I use the term ecological in its primary meaning as the relation of an organism to its environment, but also as an indication of the interdependence of all the living and nonliving systems of the earth. This vision of a planet integral with itself throughout its spatial extent and its evolutionary sequence is of primary importance if we are to have the psychic power to undergo the psychic and social transformations that are being demanded of us. These transformations require the assistance of the entire planet, not merely the forces available to the human. Otherwise we mistake the order of magnitude in this challenge.
>
> (*ibid*, 41-2)

Note the reference to "assistance of the entire planet, not merely the forces available to the human". Berry has a deep sense of the necessary inter-relationship between the human and our entire environment, both living and not living. He is asking us to enter into a humble awareness that we are a dependent species in the order of life on this planet, an awareness that can help us to step down from the arrogant posture which industrial society takes towards everything not human.

Thomas Berry is an eco theologian, a man highly regarded and widely read who sounds the tocsin to warn humanity of the complex and urgent task we face. The task is to make a successful transition from the industrial age to the ecological age. But his is not a doomsday voice. On the contrary, he sees the new cosmology, the universe story, as a liberating myth within which we can understand who we are and begin to determine what we shall do to bring the Earth and its inhabitants back from threatening ecological catastrophe. He believes that we can enter the ecological age with new energy for new spiritual achievement, towards which the universe itself urges us and itself seeks to achieve in us.

I have given attention here to Thomas Berry's views because they help to situate the task of this book. The doctrines, liturgies, ethics and organization of the Christian church all emerged two millenia ago in the context of ancient Near Eastern cosmology in which the universe was finite, Earth was its centre, and humanity was the crowning creation of the High (anthropomorphic) God. In contrast, the cosmos we are beginning to know is more extensive than we can measure and is still expanding. The ecology of Earth, our amazing island home, is being revealed as a single system made up of an undetermined number of inter-related species among which humanity is only one, though we have a special and critical function in the continuing evolution of Earth. Whatever we will mean in the future by Ultimate Reality, by Sacred Presence, within this revolutionized understanding of the cosmic context of human life, is still to be determined. And the sacred mythology by means of which humanity will express its vision of God and continue to value the life and work of Jesus of Nazareth will need new forms. A revised, dynamic faith tradition will necessarily draw upon the past, but precisely how the transition from the old to the new will happen is a large question. Thomas Berry says "We are in that phase of transition that must be described as the groping phase". (*ibid*, 47) My hope is that this book might contribute to our groping, and and I begin in the next chapters to describe those elements in the historic Hebrew-Christian faith tradition which are important to the development of the new Story.

CHAPTER SUMMARY

Human beings cannot live without sacred stories which provide each particular social group with a fabric of meanings. Such stories express in mythical terms a community's understanding of itself within the known cosmos. Each story tells a particular group who they are within the world as they know it and guides them in making decisions for their common life.

Every socially created fabric of meanings had its time of emergence and has had, or will have, its time of disintegration. This is the inevitable result of historical evolution, which brings with it deep societal change and profound alteration of how the world is understood. As existing stories die, they yield place to new ones being born.

For most of the last two millenia, the core of Western culture's fabric of meanings has been provided by the Christ Myth. This culture and its sacred myth have been gradually eroded during the last four centuries under the impact of the discoveries of science and of technological culture. We no longer have a large, credible picture, a commonly accepted world of meanings in which to place ourselves and feel at home. During the last two centuries, this loss has brought to western society a time of increasing spiritual confusion and moral decay.

Moreover, as part of this process within human consciousness there has been a gradual de-sacralizing of Earth, a widespread disrespect for the natural order. This has released an onslaught against Nature by industrial society which is unsustainable and which threatens the future of many living species, including our own.

The results of centuries of scientific discovery are giving us a basis upon which to construct a new cosmology. This cosmology embraces known reality from the smallest particles of matter/energy to the unimaginable vastness of the expanding universe. As we respond to this new cosmology we shall learn to re-imagine who we are on this planet and in this universe; we shall struggle to re-invent what it means to be human; and we shall fashion the new Story by which to guide our thoughts and feelings and actions. And Christians who continue to value their tradition have unique experience and insights to offer to this creative myth-making; they have an opportunity to share with a host of other people in the creation of a new universal humanism.

2

LEGACIES FROM ANCIENT ISRAEL

THE GEO POLITICAL WORLD OF ANCIENT ISRAEL

Within the economic, political and military realities of the ancient Near East, the territory of Syria-Canaan (today Lebanon, Syria and Palestine) was a corridor connecting three large areas of human settlement. To the north was Asia Minor, to the east were the lands of the Tigris and Euphrates rivers, and to the southwest lay Egypt, the oldest empire of the Near East. We should also mention the Mediterranean Sea to the west which periodically brought traders or invaders to the shores of Syria-Canaan. To live in the connecting corridor between these four general regions meant never to know when you would be trampled once again by an alien power eager to extend its influence and to force its way through your land seeking riches in lands beyond. That geography and those politics became the fate of the ancient Israelites; together they constituted the social and political cauldron within which Israel acquired her faith in Yahweh God.

The sacred Story recorded in the Hebrew Bible was forged within the struggles of the Hebrew people as they manoeuvered in relation to their more powerful neighbours. Their God, Yahweh, was of central importance to them because they believed that he (Yahweh was definitely male) controlled their destiny as a people. The Hebrews made no separation between their economic and political fortunes and their religious belief and practice. Yahweh was believed to govern every aspect of their social and personal existence.

As a direct consequence of that integrated awareness, every major change in the material circumstances of Israel's life was seen to involve their relationship with Yahweh. Their images of God did not originate in pious reflection but were the direct result of social, economic and political realities which they experienced. When their life was secure and rewarding, Yahweh was thanked for his blessing. When the circumstances of life deteriorated, questions surfaced about the reason for this divine judgment visited upon them by Yahweh, and about their degree of faithfulness to his will.

The ancient Hebrews looked for religious meaning in every aspect of their existence. But they did more: they created stories which revealed their experiences of the guiding and transforming Sacred Presence whom they believed was constantly shaping their history. And they recorded these stories in writings of vivid prose and poetry.

The genius of the Hebrew Bible is to be found in the fact that the people of ancient Israel had an unusual capacity for creating, telling and recording sacred stories. Most ethnic groups in human history have had oral traditions about their community life which were kept in the memory of their storytellers and were passed on from generation to generation. But the ancient Hebrews did more than remember and retell their national stories; they wrote them down, using an imaginative command of written language to produce memorable prose and poetry. Consequently, the Hebrew Bible has been able through its sacred stories to inspire the faith journeys of countless people and in its entirety became the fundamental source book of Rabbincal Judaism, Christianity and Islam.

THE GRAND NARRATIVE: ISRAEL'S NATIONAL MYTH

The Hebrew genius for storytelling can be seen in the 'Grand Narrative', an all-embracing national myth which tells about the covenants made between Yahweh and Israel. Reduced to its central core, the Grand Narrative is as follows:

- the patriarch **Abram** is addressed by God and told that he will be the father of a mighty nation (Genesis 12:1-3)
- a lasting **covenant** is made between God and Abraham (Genesis 17:1-22), whose new name means "father of many people"
- the patriarch **Jacob**, Abraham's grandson, encounters his God in a profound spiritual struggle during which his name is changed to 'Israel', meaning "he who struggles with God" (Genesis 32:22-31)
- the prophet **Moses** is addressed by God and told he will lead his people out of slavery in Egypt to possess a new land of plenty (Exodus 3:1-12)
- the enslaved group escapes the pursuing forces of pharaoh by a miraculous safe passage through an arm of the Red Sea (Exodus

21

14:5-31). Moses and the people sing a ballad celebrating their **deliverance** (Exodus 15:1-3)

- the escaped group comes to a sacred mountain in the **Sinai desert** where Moses receives from God the terms of a covenant with Israel (Exodus 19:1-6)
- the **covenant** between God and the people is sealed in the blood of oxen (Exodus 24:1-8)
- the people wander for forty years in the **wilderness**, fed by mana from heaven and given water from a rock (Exodus 16:11 - 17:7)
- Israel enters the **Promised Land** of Canaan by passing safely through the waters of the Jordan River (Joshua 3)
- under the leadership of **Joshua**, the conquest of Canaan is finally completed (Joshua 11:16-20)
- through the leadership of the prophet **Samuel**, Israel receives her first two kings, Saul (1 Samuel 10:1-8) and David (1 Samuel 16:6-13)
- God announces through the prophet Nathan that he has granted **David** an eternal covenant of blessing (2 Samuel 7:1-17)

Two features of the Grand Narrative stand out. First, there is a constant succession of fabulous manifestations of Yahweh's power and glory. This is the language of mythology. At God's behest, Egypt is attacked by a series of overwhelming plagues; sea and river are held back to serve the safety of God's people; a city wall tumbles at the blast of trumpets; a faithful donkey rebukes a fearful servant of Yahweh; armies of angels defeat Israel's enemies; Israel is wondrously fed and watered in the wilderness by gifts from Yahweh; prophets work great miracles of power and healing; and so on. While some elements of the stories obviously represent historical memory, supernatural elements are introduced to stir the imagination and win loyalty. In this way, a unique fabric of meanings is bestowed upon Israel by her Grand Narrative, a sacred mythology within which she will know her origins and understand her destiny.

The second constant feature of the Grand Narrative is the presence of Yahweh throughout the Story as the primary active agent. Though this is the Story of the birth of a nation, even more it is the Story of Yahweh

God who promises to be present in their history to achieve his purposes.

It is in the context of Israel's national myth that we encounter repeatedly a central command - the people must never forget what Yahweh has done for them. To forget is the ultimate apostasy. And, in contrast, remembering brings a deep sense of Sacred Presence within her life. The psalmists constantly repeat this theme:

> If we had forgotten the name of our God,
> > or spread out our hands to a strange god,
> would not God discover this? (44:20)

> He established a decree in Jacob,
> > and appointed a law in Israel . . .
> so that they should set their hope in God,
> > and not forget the works of God,
> > but keep his commandments. (78: 5,7)

> Bless the Lord, O my soul,
> > and do not forget all his benefits. (103:2)

> I will delight in your statutes,
> > I will not forget your word.
> > > (119:16) and many other similar texts.

We are not concerned here with a discussion of the full breadth and depth of Israel's Grand Narrative - though this is certainly a fascinating subject. Rather, we want to notice two important ways in which this national Story sets the stage for the work of Jesus of Nazareth who was himself a devout Jew and was raised in the sacred traditions of his people. We will look first at the social vision which ancient Israel developed and passed on through the generations, and then at the images of God which developed during those same centuries.

A NEW SOCIAL VISION

Jesus of Nazareth inherited from his religion and culture a specific social vision which became explicit in his public life and work. This vision had emerged centuries earlier in ancient Israel through covenant regulations by which the nation understood what Yahweh required of her - a vision of justice and compassion in social relationships and responsibilities. This vision appears, for instance, in the text designated by biblical scholars as "The Book of the Covenant": Exodus 21:1 - 23:19.

Here are a few requirements prescribed in this legislation:

"When you buy a male Hebrew slave, he shall serve six years, but in the seventh he shall go out a free person, without debt."

(21:2)

"If [a man] takes another wife to himself, he shall not diminish the food, clothing, or marital rights of the first."

(21:10)

"Whoever strikes a person mortally shall be put to death. If it was not premeditated, but came about by an act of God, then I [God] will appoint a place to which the killer may flee."

(21:12-13)

"When someone borrows an animal from another and it is injured or dies, the owner not being present, full restitution shall be made. If the owner was present, there shall be no restitution; if it was hired, only the hiring fee is due."

(22:14-15)

"You shall not wrong or oppress a resident alien, for you were aliens in the land of Egypt. You shall not abuse any widow or orphan."

(22:21-22)

"If you lend money to my people, to the poor among you, you shall not deal with them as a creditor; you shall not exact interest from them. If you take your neighbour's cloak in pawn, you shall restore it before the sun goes down; for it may be your neighbour's only clothing to use as a cover; in what else shall that person sleep? And if your neighbour cries out to me, I will listen, for I am compassionate."

(22:25-27)

"You shall not spread a false report. You shall not join hands with the wicked to act as a malicious witness. You shall not follow a majority in wrong-doing; when you bear witness in a law suit, you shall not side with the majority so as to pervert justice; nor shall you be partial to the poor in a lawsuit."

(23:1-3)

"You shall not pervert the justice due to your poor in their lawsuits."

(23:6)

"For six years you shall sow your land and gather its yield; but the seventh year you shall let it rest and lie fallow, so that the poor of your people may eat; and what they leave the wild animals may eat. You shall do the same with your vineyard, and with your olive orchard."

(23:10-11)

This sampling indicates the kind of relationships considered to be just. The regulations set out rights for members of the believing community which are not subject to the whim of any human overlord because they represent the will of Yahweh. They also indicate a concern for people who come upon hard times, people who through no fault of their own become socially or economically marginalized. This communal justice is to be marked with compassion, a quality which Israel first encountered in Yahweh's revealing words to Moses in Midian:

> I have observed the misery of my people who are in Egypt; I have heard their cry on account of their taskmasters. Indeed, I know their sufferings, and I have come down to deliver them from the Egyptians, and to bring them up out of that land to a good and broad land, a land flowing with milk and honey.
>
> (Exodus 3:7-8)

We go next to the Book Deuteronomy which was written in the seventh century BCE as a kind of 'constitution' for Israel, to make her a people dedicated to Yahweh. Here also we find key legislation which requires personal righteousness and social justice. These qualities had been stressed by the great prophets of the preceding century, harking back to still older traditions ascribed to Moses. From Deuteronomy, here is sample legislation:

> "Every seventh year you shall grant a remission of debts. And this is the manner of the remission: every creditor shall remit the claim that is held against a neighbour, not exacting it of a neighbour who is a member of the community, because the Lord's remission has been proclaimed. . . . There will, however, be no one in need among you, because the Lord is sure to bless you in the land that the Lord your God is giving you as a possession to occupy."
>
> (Dt. 15:1,2,4)

> "If there is among you anyone in need, a member of your community in any of your towns within the land that the Lord your God is giving you, do not be hard-hearted or tight-fisted toward your neighbour. You should rather

open your hand, willingly lending enough to meet the need, whatever it may be. Be careful that you do not entertain a mean thought, thinking, 'The seventh year, the year of remission, is near,' and therefore view your needy neighbour with hostility and give nothing; . . . . Since there will never cease to be some in need on the earth, I therefore command you, 'Open your hand to the poor and needy neighbour in your land."

(Dt. 15:7-11)

"And when you send a male slave out from you a free person, you shall not send him out empty-handed. Provide liberally out of your flock, your threshing floor, and your wine press, thus giving to him some of the bounty with which the Lord your God has blessed you."

Dt. 15:12-14)

"You shall appoint judges and officials throughout your tribes, in all your towns that the Lord your God is giving to you, and they shall render just decisions for the people. You must not distort justice; you must not show partiality; and you must not accept bribes, for a bribe blinds the eyes of the wise and subverts the cause of those who are in the right. Justice, and only justice, you shall pursue, so that you may live and occupy the land that the Lord your God is giving you."

(Dt. 16:18-20)

"One of your own community you may set as king over you . . . . he must not acquire many horses for himself . . . . he must not acquire many wives for himself . . . . silver and gold he must not acquire in great quantity for himself. When he has taken the throne of his kingdom, he shall have a copy of this law written for him in the presence of the levitical priests. It shall remain with him and he shall read in it all the days of his life, so that he may learn to fear the Lord his God, diligently observing all the words of this law and these statutes."

(Dt. 17:15ff)

This small selection of texts indicates the kind of personal righteousness and social compassion required of all the citizens in this small Near Eastern land of Judah. Later in this chapter we shall hear from some of the great prophets who chastized Israel for forsaking the ways of the Mosaic covenant and who demanded a return to the social vision the nation had received. And centuries after those prophets, when Jesus of Nazareth appeared in Roman Palestine as a successor to the prophets, he reaffirmed the social vision.

AN IMAGE OF GOD AS POWERFUL

Ancient Israel was a people rooted in the conviction that her God Yahweh exercised divine power for her benefit alone. She held a vision of the Holy One which was strongly nationalistic. In the books of Numbers, Joshua and Judges, for example, we find stories of the 'settlement tradition' which tell how Israel occupied the land of Canaan. In these narratives we meet the Warrior God whom Israel believed went with her armies and dealt harshly with her enemies. This image of Yahweh as a warrior was appropriated from Canaanite mythology and his active presence on behalf of the chosen people is clearly represented in some of the psalms:

> He provides food for those who fear him;
>   he is ever mindful of his covenant.
> He has shown his people the power of his works,
>   in giving them the heritage of the nations.
>
> (Psalm 111:5-6)

> In Judah God is known, his name is great in Israel.
>   His abode has been established in Salem,
> his dwelling place in Zion.
>   There he broke the flashing arrows, the shield, the
> sword, and the weapons of war.
>
> (Psalm 76:1-3)

> [Yahweh said] "Mark this, then, you who forget God,
>   or I will tear you apart, and there will be no one to
>   deliver.
> Those who bring thanksgiving honor me."
>
> (Psalm 50:22)

Yahweh, the Warrior God, demanded appropriate sacrifices if his cult was to remain efficacious. In the ancient Near Eastern world, thanksgiving through ritual sacrifice to the gods was practised to obtain divine favour and to avoid divine wrath. Israel's Warrior God emerged within this cultural tradition. But alongside this awe-filled 'fear of the Lord' and a gratitude for his works done for Israel, a moral and spiritual 'covenant faithfulness' gradually gained in importance. The observance of God's laws, as laid out in social legislation similar to that mentioned above, ultimately became the principal means by which Israel hoped to retain the divine blessing. As the image of the warrior god faded, a God of covenant faithfulness developed to replace it.

Yahweh was the One who "was giving the land" for his people to occupy. Not only by sacrifice but by moral living was Israel to retain Yahweh's blessing. Yahweh was indeed the powerful God who would guide and defend his people; but they, for their part, must never forget the works of God in their midst and must obey his commands. And beyond moral requirements, there was a dawning awareness that they were to learn the meaning of love between Yahweh and Israel. This became explicit in the oracles of Hosea the prophet, where the nation is seen as the beloved bride of Yahweh.

The nation's self-confidence as the chosen people of Yahweh became seriously undermined, however, as Israel experienced repeated defeats at the hands of imperial enemies. Assyria in the 8th century conquered the ten northern tribes; Babylon in the 6th century devastated Judah, leaving Jerusalem in ruins and the temple destroyed. Subsequently, Persians and Greeks became overlords of the remnant people, now known as Judahites or Jews. As a result of these national misfortunes, the mood in Israel changed dramatically. Some of the psalms lament Israel's fate and wonder aloud about God's presence in the nation:

> O God, the nations have come into your inheritance;
>> they have defiled your holy temple;
>> they have laid Jerusalem in ruins.
> They have given the bodies of your servants
>> to the birds of the air for food,
>> the flesh of your faithful to the wild animals of the earth.
> Do not remember against us the iniquities of our
>> ancestors;
>> let your compassion come speedily to meet us,
>> for we are brought very low.
>
> (Psalm 79:1,2,8)

With the coming of national humiliation, a wide-ranging debate troubled Israel as she wondered about the state of her covenant with Yahweh. This debate was reflected in late Jewish writing, as for example in the Book of Job.

Job, a righteous and good man, is grievously afflicted by the death of his children and the loss of his personal well-being. He curses the day of his birth. Four self-appointed and self-righteous counsellors visit Job to explain how, given the terrible circumstances of his life, he must have sinned grievously. Each of them gives counsel as to how Job must seek to amend his life and his relationship with Yahweh. But the speeches of Job's 'comforters' leave him unconvinced about God's good will, and in his desperation Job challenges God to demonstrate his purported justice. Only a divine theophany (a manifestation of divine power) causes Job to repent in dust and ashes.

The author of this writing creates a classic study of what happens to religious faith under the onslaught of devastating human suffering and despair. He gives literary expression to a theological debate within Israel arising from her acute national afflictions. The story reflects different perceptions within the nation of how suffering affected faith in Yahweh. The thorny question of what can be meant by 'God's power in history' had entered Hebrew religion and has never left it since that time.

Late in biblical Israel's history, in the fifth century BCE, the scribe and law-giver Ezra took action to strengthen Israel's identity and self-confidence as Yahweh's chosen people. With his emphasis on the Law, on Torah, he tried to 'circle the wagons', to defend the chosen people against contamination from abroad. He did this chiefly by requiring all male Jews to put away their foreign wives which they had acquired during the decades of mixing with other ethnic groups. This insistence on Jewish self-awareness and exclusiveness became a powerful weapon for the preservation of coming generations of Jews. In the fourth century the world of the Near East and beyond became subject to the tide of Hellenization, the powerful and persuasive influence of classical Greek culture. Ezra's reforms helped the nation to retain the ancient Hebrew spirit of intolerance for any deviation from exclusive loyalty to Yahweh.

On the other hand, this same demand for exclusive loyalty triggered a strong reaction in the form of satirical criticism by another Jewish scribe, the author of the Book of Jonah. This book was written to attack Israel's spiritual arrogance and self-importance which had followed upon the times of Ezra. In this story - which has been called a cartoon - the devout Jew, Jonah, is told by God to preach repentance and faith to the foreign city of Nineveh. When, as an exclusionary believer, he refuses the divine command and runs away to sea, Jonah is tossed overboard from the escape ship and is taken into the belly of a whale appointed by God to receive him. When the whale spits Jonah on to the shore, he continues very reluctantly on his divinely appointed journey and arrives finally at Nineveh where he preaches the need for the city to repent. When the amazingly pious city responds to God's Word and repents in sackcloth and ashes, Jonah is furious with God. As the author comments, Jonah sulked: "It is better for me to die than to live."

To view the story as history completely misses the point being made by the anonymous prophetic writer. Jonah is symbolic of Israel and Nineveh is symbolic of foreigners (Nineveh had been the capital of the now defunct Assyrian Empire). In this cartoon, Israel is spoofed as faithless precisely because of her arrogant self-assurance of being God's chosen people. The author mocks Israel for clutching God's blessing to herself and being unwilling to share it beyond her borders. The writer of the Book of Jonah condemns the narrow nationalism in Israel's faith just as strongly as other prophetic writers had condemned the nation for her neglect of justice, righteousness and compassion. This prophet's image of God was revolutionary: Yahweh is compassionate to all people of all nations. The stage was being set for the work of Jesus of Nazareth.

AN IMAGE OF GOD AS COMPASSIONATE

When discussing the images of power used by Israel to speak of her God, mention was made of teachings by the great prophets which modified the understanding of divine wrath and asserted divine compassion. We return now in more detail to this issue.

In the tenth to eighth centuries BCE, when the ten northern tribes of Israel were growing in power and regional significance, the sacrificial system at the heart of the worship of Yahweh became a source of glaring hypocrisy. A blasphemous dichotomy developed between widespread public injustice and personal immorality on the one hand, and the practice of cultic sacrifice on the other hand. The priesthood of the official cult of Yahweh proclaimed that observance of the cult was adequate to maintain covenant faithfulness, while at the same time no effort was made to keep the heart of Yahweh's Law in social justice and personal righteousness. A profound hypocrisy festered in the heart of the nation.

Against this widespread moral decay and hypocritical religion, prophets of both Israel (in the north) and Judea (in the south) spoke the Word of the Lord:

> I hate, I despise your festivals,
> and I take no delight in your solemn assemblies.
> Even though you offer me your burnt offerings and grain
> offerings, I will not accept them. . .
> Take away from me the noise of your songs;
> I will not listen to the melody of your harps.
> But let justice roll down like waters,
> and righteousness like an ever-flowing stream.
>
> (Amos 5:21-24)
>
> Will the Lord be pleased with thousands of rams,
> with ten thousands of rivers of oil?
> Shall I give my firstborn for my transgression,
> the fruit of my body for the sin of my soul?
> He has told you, O mortal, what is good;
> and what does the Lord require of you
> but to do justice, and to love kindness,
> and to walk humbly with your God?
>
> (Micah 6:7-8)
>
> When you come to appear before me,
> who asked this from your hand?
> Trample my courts no more: bringing offerings is futile. . .
> learn to do good; seek justice, rescue the oppressed,
> defend the orphan, plead for the widow.
>
> (Isaiah 1:12,17)

Israel's prophets recalled and deepened the social vision which was already present in Israel from the Mosaic covenant tradition. Eighth century prophets urged their societies to follow the ways of justice and compassion and warned that failure to observe the covenant would bring national disaster. There was, however, more to the prophetic vision of God than a divine righteousness and wrath against sin. The prophet Hosea of Israel came to a profound conviction that there was in Yahweh's heart an insistent compassion:

> How can I give you up, Ephraim?
> How can I hand you over, O Israel?. . .
> My heart recoils within me;
> my compassion grows warm and tender.

31

I will not execute my fierce anger; I will not again destroy
    Ephraim; for I am God and no mortal,
the Holy One in your midst, and I will not come in wrath.

(Hosea ll:8-9)

The cry of the prophet articulates the compassion which he believes lives in the heart of Yahweh.

Some years later the prophet Isaiah of Jerusalem in Judea testified to his own personal experience of God's searching forgiveness. He received an inner cleansing which was so complete that it freed him to take up the difficult task of challenging his people to renounce their rebellious ways.

> In the year that King Uzziah died, I saw the Lord sitting on a throne, high and lofty; and the hem of his robe filled the temple. Seraphs were in attendance above him; each had six wings: with two they covered their faces, and with two they covered their feet, and with two they flew. And one called to another and said:
>   "Holy, holy, holy is the Lord of Hosts;
>   the whole earth is full of his glory."
> The pivots on the thresholds shook at the voices of those who called, and the house filled with smoke. And I said: "Woe is me! I am lost, for I am a man of unclean lips, and I live among a people of unclean lips. . . . Then one of the seraphs flew to me, holding a live coal that had been taken from the altar with a pair of tongs. The seraph touched my mouth with it and said: "Now that this has touched your lips, your guilt has departed and your sin is blotted out." Then I heard the voice of the Lord saying, "Whom shall I send, and who will go for us?" And I said, "Here am I; send me!"

(Isa 6:1-8)

Without being required to make any act of propitiation to God for his own sin and for the sin of his people, Isaiah is released from his interior bondage.

The same insight and conviction found its way, here and there, into the songs of Israel's worship:

> For you have no delight in sacrifice;
>   if I were to give a burnt offering,
>   you would not be pleased.
> The sacrifice acceptable to God is a broken spirit;

> a broken and contrite heart,
> O God, you will not despise.

(Psalm 51:16-17)

Psalm 40:6-7 has the same conviction expressed with a further significant affirmation:

> Sacrifice and offering you do not desire,
>> but you have given me an open ear.
> Burnt offering and sin offering you have not required.
>> Then I said, "Here I am . . .

These psalmists have realized that contrition for sin and sincere intention to learn the ways of obedience to the divine Word are sufficient to bring faithful people into that life-giving exchange of love which the Holy One seeks with his beloved people. The singers are able to proclaim in great simplicity and confidence before their God, 'Here I am'. The compassionate God will hear and respond. Psalms 103 and 65 express similar sentiments:

> Bless the Lord, O my soul,
>> and do not forget all his benefits -
>> who forgives all your iniquity,
>> who heals all your diseases. . . .
> The Lord is merciful and gracious,
>> slow to anger and abounding in steadfast love.
> He will not always accuse
>> nor will he keep his anger forever.
> He does not deal with us according to our sins,
>> nor repay us according to our iniquities.
> For as the heavens are high above the earth,
>> so great is his steadfast love toward those
>> who fear him;
> as far as the east is from the west,
>> so far he removes our transgressions from us.

(103:2,3,8-12)

> Praise is due to you, O God, in Zion;
>> and to you shall vows be performed,
>> O you who answer prayer!
> To you all flesh shall come.
>> When deeds of iniquity overwhelm us,
>> you forgive our transgressions.

(65:1-3)

Psalm 139 shows us a reach of spiritual understanding and beauty seldom achieved elsewhere in the Hebrew Scriptures:

> Where can I go from your spirit?
>> Or where can I flee from your presence?
> If I ascend to heaven, you are there;
>> if I make my bed in Sheol, you are there.
> If I take the wings of the morning
>> and settle at the farthest limits of the sea,
> even there your hand shall lead me,
>> and your right hand shall hold me fast.
> If I say, "Surely the darkness will cover me,
>> and the light around me become night,"
> even the darkness is not dark to you;
>> the night is as bright as the day,
>> for the darkness is as light to you.

(139:7-12)

These visions of divine compassion and companionship conflict with affirmations about Yahweh found elsewhere in the Hebrew Scriptures. Yahweh is represented frequently as arbitrary in action, demanding punishment for sin, and withholding forgiveness until proper ritual atonement is made. In her early teachings Israel drew from religious traditions, common throughout the Near East, which asserted that the gods demanded sacrificial worship to obtain their good will. But Israel, unlike her neighbours, was on an unusual and lengthy spiritual journey. In prophetic oracles and psalm verses we meet convictions which emerged alongside, and sought to replace, previous teaching about the necessity for propitiatory sacrifice. Some of Israel's sensitive souls were finding alternative images of God's relationship to the nation. This alternative view called Israel to new spiritual heights which she did not fully attain until after the emergence of Rabbinical Judaism late in the first century of the Common Era.

Biblical Israel, however, never entirely set aside her original cult traditions in which sacrificial worship and its theological foundations had a central place. Thus both images of God - the early and the later, the ancient and the prophetic, the wrathful and the compassionate - are evident in Israel's sacred Scriptures. In the times of Jesus of Nazareth there remained an unresolved tension between them.

CHAPTER SUMMARY

The land of the ancient Hebrews was placed within the political geography of the Near East as a corridor through which the armies of her powerful neighbours frequently marched in conflict with one another. The repeated tribulations resulting from this circumstance dramatically affected the development of Israel's religious self-understanding. Whatever happened to Israel as a nation was believed to be directly under the governance of her God Yahweh. Her religious self-understanding was worked out within the political and economic realities of her national experience.

Ancient Israel's long experience of repeated social, political and military struggle resulted in a national memory of heroic sagas which were remembered and recited in sacred stories. The repeated oral retelling of these stories was eventually transformed by skilled writers into the sacred text which we know as the Hebrew Bible. At the core of this sacred text is Israel's Grand Narrative, a sequence of sacred stories which portrays the nation's origins and destiny as the chosen people of her national God, Yahweh. This unified sacred Story is largely mythological in form and content, a dramatic fabric of meanings which provided the people with self-understanding.

Two aspects of Israel's Grand Narrative are of particular importance to the argument of this book. The first is a social vision which is laid out in the Mosaic law code and elaborated by the greatest of the Hebrew prophets. Personal righteousness and social justice are the cornerstones of this vision, with special emphasis on compassionate care for the marginalized members of that society.

The second aspect of the Grand Narrative to which we give special attention here is the evolution of Israel's image of her God. In Israel's beginnings, Yahweh was a Warrior God who was believed to act in defence of the safety and interests of his people. But as Israel struggled to comprehend her own national tribulation and suffering she came to an understanding of the divine compassion. The power of Yahweh was now seen as the strength of his forgiving and healing love for Israel, a view which then existed in tension with earlier convictions about the power of Yahweh to defeat his - and Israel's - enemies.

This distinction and tension marked the religion of biblical Israel and was part of the religious legacy inherited by Jesus of Nazareth.

3

A PROPHET IN GALILEE

> He was a spirit person, subversive sage, social prophet,
> and movement founder who invited his followers and
> hearers into a transforming relationship with the same
> Spirit that he himself knew, and into a community whose
> social vision was shaped by the core value of
> compassion.
>
> (Marcus Borg,
> "Meeting Jesus Again for the First Time", 119)

Jesus of Nazareth was a first century Jew. He grew up and was nurtured within the cultural traditions of the Hebrew people and he shared in their everyday experience of oppression under Roman imperial rule. The temple in Jerusalem was the central symbol of the Jews' faith in Yahweh but, for the peasant majority, village gatherings for Torah instruction were their immediate source of spiritual and moral counsel. These gatherings or 'synagogues' (lit: coming together) were assemblies where the people met with their local religious leaders; synagogues were physical structures only in major centres. Thus, in the small village of Nazareth, as well as in the intimate nurture of his home, Jesus (as Luke says) "grew and became strong, filled with wisdom; and the favour of God was upon him."

BAPTISM

> John the baptizer appeared in the wilderness,
> proclaiming a baptism of repentance for the forgiveness
> of sins. And people from the whole Judean countryside
> and all the people of Jerusalem were going out to him,
> and were confessing their sins. . . . In those days Jesus
> came from Nazareth of Galilee and was baptized by John
> in the Jordan. And just as he was coming up out of the
> water, he saw the heavens torn apart and the Spirit
> descending like a dove on him. And a voice came from
> heaven, "You are my Son, the Beloved; with you I am well
> pleased." And the Spirit immediately drove him out into
> the wilderness.
>
> (Mark 1:4-5, 9-12)

37

Traditional Christian teaching has seldom if ever placed emphasis on Jesus' baptism as an event critically important for his life work. On the other hand, the words, "You are my Son, the Beloved", carry the marks of a very early Christian naming of Jesus and as such have received much attention. This naming has been used to support the doctrine of Jesus as the Son of God, a doctrine which was placed at the heart of the Church's teaching. But Jesus' baptism itself has not been seen as indicating a fundamental turning point in his life. This seems strange when we consider what preceded and followed that event, and the nature of the experience itself.

From where had Jesus come to be baptized? Mark says, "from Nazareth", from his home village, from the years of early growth and social formation, from his work as a carpenter, from his socially assigned place in a poor Jewish village community. There, too, he would have drawn deeply from his people's extensive spiritual tradition. Those early years marked him for the rest of his life.

When Jesus heard about John, he left home along with the crowds who were responding to the Baptist's message. We cannot know with certainty what motivated Jesus to do this. However, considering information in Jewish writings of the previous two centuries, we are justified in believing that Jesus, steeped in his people's faith tradition, was looking eagerly for signs that the God of Israel was again stirring in the midst of the chosen people. For at least two centuries the Jews had engaged in apocalyptic yearnings, looking for Yahweh to come in judgment and mighty power upon their enemies and to establish Jerusalem as the centre of the world. When Jesus of Nazareth went to John at the river, he was well prepared in heart, mind and will to receive a divine summons to do the will of the God of Israel.

The immediate effect upon Jesus of his baptism by John cannot be described in detail but only surmised. "He saw the heavens torn apart and the Spirit descending like a dove on him. And a voice came from heaven . . ." Considering all that was to follow in the life of this man, this symbolic record of human/Divine encounter is surely one of the most restrained in all the biblical records. In this modest account we have a sacred story as significant for the Christian Story as was the story of

Moses and the burning bush for the Hebrew Story.

"And the Spirit immediately drove him out into the wilderness". Another understatement. Even when we acknowledge that Jesus' years in Nazareth had prepared him for that moment at the river Jordan, we can barely imagine the depth of spiritual transformation which made it impossible for him to return to Nazareth. He could not return to his accustomed life because there was a new, imperative work to be assigned by the Word of Yahweh. And there was only one place to go to hear that Word: into the wilderness, to ponder and to pray and to plan, like so many of the great Hebrew prophets before him. There was no option, no question of resuming life as usual. The road ahead was new, it was necessary, and it was unmarked.

Matthew (4:1-11) and Luke (4:1-13) report that in the wilderness Jesus experienced temptations from Satan. The story suggests that Jesus was wrestling with options concerning how he would undertake the work ahead. In this profound spiritual struggle he chose not to provide his people with material security, not to perform stunning wonderworks, and not to seek political power. On the other hand, nothing is said in this story about what Jesus did see as his path ahead. For that story the evangelists invite us to read on into their gospels and to watch Jesus in his public words and deeds.

Judging from its consequences for humanity, the experience of being baptized by John and then being driven into the wilderness was for Jesus a human/Divine encounter such as the world rarely sees. We are again, as in the story of Moses, at one of the major turning points in human history.

TEACHING ABOUT GOD

In the gospels, Jesus' understanding of God is best drawn from his actions and parables because his direct teaching has few explicit references to the character of the Holy One. In these actions and stories we find consistently revealed a God who is compassionate, vulnerable and generous, the same image of God which earlier we found in parts of the prophetic tradition of his people. This prophetic image is elaborated in Jesus' famous parable of a father and two sons (Luke 15:11-32).

As the story begins, the younger son asks for his share of the family estate and then goes away and spends it in riotous living. In a far country he is reduced to the role of swineherd, "and he would gladly have fed on the pods that the swine ate; and no one gave him anything". We are presented with a young man alienated from family and community, and left with little or no self-esteem. He feels utterly lost and ultimately decides there is nothing to lose by going home.

As he makes his way back, he constantly rehearses words of penitence and confession: "'Father, I have sinned against heaven and before you; I am no longer worthy to be called your son; treat me as one of your hired servants'. . . . But while he was yet at a distance, his father saw him and had compassion, and ran and embraced him and kissed him". In that moment of meeting, when the penitent son finally has the opportunity to speak his well rehearsed lines, the father does not even notice what is being said.

It seems evident that in the son's absence, the father had suffered terrible anguish. His heart was filled with compassion and forgiveness. This is a parent who grieves for the waywardness of a child and who does not cast himself in the role of victim of his son's behaviour. The father is not occupied in blaming the absent son for his behaviour, nor in nursing vindictive thoughts; he waits eagerly to do his part in a reconciliation, whenever the son may have a change of heart and return home. Thus, when the son appears on the distant horizon, the father doesn't wait for a disgraced and penitent youth to come to the house and grovel before him. "While he was still far off" (this is not an accidental detail in Jesus' story but is intended to stress the father's enduring compassionate love throughout the son's absence), the father jumps to his feet, runs to meet him, and in great joy unceremoniously hugs the delinquent. He calls the servants and orders a great feast which is to be held in celebration of the younger son's return.

And what of the penitent son? What is his experience as he becomes aware of his father's amazing love? The parable strongly suggests that without any hesitation the son accepts the loving forgiveness being offered and immediately becomes reconciled with his father. We, the listeners, rejoice that he is no longer separated from his family and we are led to expect that this familial healing will place him once again in the larger community where he can resume normal living. A wonderful and generous gift of suffering love, given by the father and accepted by the son, accomplishes a transformation in the young man's life. The father, at a cost to himself of personal anguish and sorrow which he gladly endured, extends unconditional acceptance toward the one whom he dearly loves. This costly love completes a transformation in the son which had begun in his contrition. Indeed, it seems likely that the son's decision to return home had been directly related to his memory of earlier experiences of the father's love.

There is little need to comment further on the point of Jesus' story. It must be taken as a parable of the depths of God's love for wayward humanity, a God who extends a generous love to us even before we become aware that we need it.

Jesus continues his story. While the younger son is away squandering money and time, an older brother has dutifully stayed at home and helped his father run the farm. When he learns of the father's actions for the prodigal son, he is outraged. It is beyond his comprehension that the renegade should be accepted back. He does not understand anything of the father's love toward the younger son. And what is worse, he has never been able to see or accept the depth of the father's love for himself. "Listen", he says to his father, "For all these years I have been working like a slave for you, and I have never disobeyed your command; yet you have never given me even a goat so that I might celebrate with my friends." This son only knows about earning his keep. He had been so little aware of the father's love for him that he had never thought to ask for anything so extravagant as a party for his friends. It had never occured to this young man that he is constantly being held by a love which is recklessly generous. We as listeners feel sadness for his continuing alienation from the greatest gift he could ever be offered or accept. Will he never see, understand and accept the gift which he needs more than anything else?

To feel the spiritual depths of this parable, we must keep before us the contrast which Jesus portrays between the behaviour of the two sons, and the single-minded and identical behaviour of the father in his actions toward them both. As is true of all Jesus' parables, the story is painted in bold, simple strokes so that the meaning is set out in the contrasting characters and how they act. Here we see a father who loves both his sons equally and two sons whose responses are opposite. For the one it means a joyful redirecting of his life; for the other it means confusion and resentment in the face of an unqualified generosity he is not able to understand nor accept, neither for himself nor for his brother.

The parable teaches nothing, however, about responsibilities which follow for those who do accept such a gift. There were other occasions when Jesus spoke about the cost of discipleship. Here, in this story, he is underlining the priority of receiving.

In passing, notice that Jesus is not teaching that God is to be imaged as a father figure. If women and not men had been the customary landowners and powerbrokers, and Jesus had told his story about a mother and two sons, he would not thereby have meant that God is to be imaged as a mother. Divine compassion and generosity are not gendered.

Jesus' teaching about God's generous love which waits for our acceptance is also apparent in his actions. John's gospel, Chapter 13, recounts an episode which takes place during the last meal with the twelve. We are told that during supper Jesus "got up from the table, took off his outer robe, and tied a towel around himself. Then he poured water into a basin and began to wash the disciples feet." Peter protested when Jesus came to him, "Lord, are you going to wash my feet? . . . You will never wash my feet." Jesus answered, "Unless I wash you, you have no share with me." Jesus' meaning is clear: unless you, Peter, can accept from me the love I have to give to you, you cannot be my disciple.

Receiving the love which God has to give us is a prerequisite for living the new life of discipleship. Jesus' God gives, and gives generously; as we learn to accept this gift we grow in understanding of what God expects of us. Jesus' God is intimately engaged with us in the journey to become the person we are meant to be, and for the sake of the work we are called to do.

This latter point is emphasized in an encounter between Jesus and a man who had "many possessions". The story is recorded in all three

Synoptic gospels (Mk 10:17-22; Mt 19:16-22, Lk 18:18-23). As the story begins, a man runs up and kneels before Jesus, suggesting to the reader that there is some urgency in his errand. His words tell us what that errand was: "Good Teacher, what must I do to inherit eternal life?" Jesus responds by leading the man into a discussion about keeping the Torah, which reveals something about the man's character and intentions.

This part of the conversation, however, is inconclusive. The man observes that he has "kept all these" commandments since his youth, but has come to Jesus for something more. Mark makes it clear that the man, having done everything required of him by the Jewish religion, is left with the feeling that there is still more for him to do. Mark comments, "Jesus, looking at him, loved him". Then, accepting at face value the man's stated intention, Jesus responded with a challenging proposal: "You lack one thing; go, sell what you own, and give the money to the poor, and you will have treasure in heaven; then come, follow me." There was, undoubtedly, a shocked silence. The man left "grieving, for he had many possessions."

One aspect of this encounter reveals Jesus' requirement of people with status in that society who wanted to work with him: they must abandon their class privileges and give their wealth to the poor. But in addition, let us notice that Jesus' words, "Follow me", held a gift, a promise. At the very least, to follow the Teacher would bring this man the wondrous gifts of Jesus' close companionship, friendship and love. The man was not being given a bald, unsupported challenge; there was an assurance in Jesus' person and words that the man would receive the necessary inner strength and outer help if he chose to become a follower. It was a choice which he could actually make if he were open to the gifts which accompanied the challenge. Mark tells us, however, that the man was aghast at the proposed material sacrifice. He was being invited to become one of the poor "for my sake and the gospel" and he could discern nothing beyond the loss of his wealth. Vividly seeing the cost, he failed to see the gift. He was possessed by his possessions and the only way to escape from that prison was beyond his ability to accomplish.

The evangelists, in these stories and in many others, present actions and parables of Jesus which in effect reveal Jesus' image of the Holy One. The stories reveal both an amazing divine generosity and a vulnerability intrinsic to that generosity. The prodigal son could have selfishly exploited his father's forgiveness; the twelve close friends of Jesus might have refused the washing of their feet and all that this implied about God's gifts for them; the young man in fact refused the way of life being offered to him. Are we to say then that it is a foolish and weak God who offers love unconditionally to humankind and in so doing becomes vulnerable to our refusals? Or, is there within that apparent divine foolishness and weakness a hidden wisdom and a hidden strength? In the next chapter we will consider the answer which Paul the Apostle gave to this question.

TO BE A NEIGHBOUR

The Hebrew prophets claimed that one essential element in human response to the Divine is, as Micah says, "to do justice, and to love kindness, and to walk humbly with your God". The prophets spoke the Word of the Lord against Israel's social and personal sin and called for the people to learn the ways of mutual service in justice, righteousness and compassion. Jesus of Nazareth built upon that prophetic faith, insight and conviction whenever he invited people into more creative forms of community living. We notice in the gospels that Jesus turned people towards one another in mutual awareness and caring; this was the first and principal consequence of knowing themselves to be people of God. Not to respond to the needs of others was to abandon faith in the Holy One. A prime example of this central message is Jesus' parable of the good Samaritan (Luke 10:29-37).

Luke, editor of this text, provides a preface and a conclusion to this parable in the form of exchanges between Jesus and a lawyer. It is Luke's way of bringing out the central thrust of the story itself. So we must take note of these opening and closing exchanges as they provide the essential clue for understanding Jesus' story.

To begin, the lawyer asks Jesus, "Who is my neighbour?" And between the lines we hear his meaning: 'Which of the many people I

44

encounter in my daily life does the commandment require me to love? Whom must I care for and whom can I leave aside? Who is my neighbour and who is not my neighbour?'

Jesus does not give a direct answer to the lawyer's question. Instead he tells a story about a man on the road from Jerusalem to Jericho who falls among robbers who beat and rob him and leave him for dead by the roadside. Two clergy of the local religious establishment pass by on the other side of the road because they fear the grievous ritual impurity which would come upon them from associating with what appears to be a dead body. But a third man, a Samaritan, and therefore an 'outsider' to all good Jews, came upon the injured man, bound up his wounds, lifted him on to his donkey and delivered him to an inn, saying to the innkeeper, "Take care of him; and when I come back, I will repay you whatever more you spend".

Luke then tells us that Jesus, having concluded his story, turned to the lawyer with a question that is different from the question which the lawyer had asked Jesus earlier. "Which of these three, do you think, was a neighbour to the man who fell into the hands of the robbers?" The lawyer's question had been: "Who is my neighbour?", as though seeking a list of people he must treat kindly. Jesus' question asks about the condition of the man's heart: Are you ready to be a neighbour? The man's question was built around a noun, "neighbour". Jesus' question was built around a verb, "to be a neighbour".

The way in which Luke frames the story with two very different questions indicates that he sees Jesus making a revolutionary change in the second of the two great commandments of Jewish tradition, "You shall love the Lord your God, and your neighbour as yourself". It had been well understood for centuries among Jews that this commandment applied only within the Jewish community. In contrast, Jesus implies: "You shall love the Lord your God, and then you will be able to respond as a compassionate neighbour to those in need ". Jesus asks: "Are you ready to be a neighbour whenever the need arises?" Jesus says: "Let your response to human need be recklessly generous, even as God is recklessly generous in response to your needs." Jesus constantly drew upon his God as the Sacred Ground of his own life for resources he

45

needed to do the will of the Holy One. And he urged others to discover this truth in their own lives. Doing this, they would discover resources to be a neighbour.

We might, then, offer this as a summary of Jesus' counsel:

In this world, all is Gift.

Receive what you need with gratitude,

give to others' needs with generosity.

In the parable of the Good Samaritan, Jesus is seeking transformation of the human heart. He wants to deliver us from a deep fear, the fear that we may have too many demands placed on us, the fear that our frail love and limited resources will be overtaxed. He counters this fear by assuring that in opening ourselves to Sacred Presence, wherever and however we experience this, we shall receive what we need in order to be able to respond to others' needs. As we, in our need, learn to open ourselves to receive gifts of life which can be ours, as we nourish our awareness of the Sacred around and within us, we shall have the wisdom and the resources to act in love towards others.

This conviction and practice was central to Jesus' life and teaching. He chose to be a neighbour and he opened his life to Sacred Presence to receive the strength to do so. Occasionally the evangelists show Jesus going off by himself to lonely places to be solitary, to renew his inner life. For Jesus, the Holy One is the constant divine Companion on life's dusty road. The Holy One is a Mystery of Lowliness who abides with us, to be each person's inner strength and to enable each person's neighbourly work. A sense of the Sacred is a fundamental human resource for creative living.

Jesus' own sense of the Sacred within the natural order is revealed in words ascribed to him:

Look at the birds of the air; they neither sow nor reap nor gather into barns, and yet your heavenly father feeds them. Are you not of more value than they? And can any of you by worrying add a single hour to your span of life? And why do you worry about clothing? Consider the lilies of the field, how they grow; they neither toil nor spin, yet I tell you even Solomon in all his glory was not clothed like one of these.

(Matt 6:26-29)

We do not know in what way Jesus responded to the rapacious actions of his contemporaries in deforestation and other destructive agricultural practices. The evangelists have their attention turned in other directions. Yet one of his most famous disciples, Francis of Assisi, is renowned for his nature mysticism. It is not unreasonable to suppose that Jesus was open to the wonders of the world around him and to its gifts for spiritual life just as much as he was attentive to the presence of the Sacred within himself and within other people.

JESUS OF NAZARETH'S CHOICE

> If we are to say that religion cannot be concerned with politics, then we are really saying that there is a substantial part of human life in which God's writ does not run. If it is not God's, then whose is it?
>
> Archbishop Desmond Tutu

Roman Palestine was a deeply troubled land in the first century CE. Ninety percent of the population were peasants who were subject to a four-fold oppression: imperial Rome, the temple authorities in Jerusalem, the carefully stratified social system which assigned dominant status to the upper classes, and rigorous Jewish religious practices which were beyond the capacity of most peasants to observe.

Roman occupation meant a constant threat of the use of military force, should the populace cause an undesirable disturbance. But the imperial tribute, imposed as a tax on all agricultural produce, was even more burdensome. Temple authorities also imposed a tax, and religious duty brought with it the obligation of tithing. In all, the peasantry stood to lose to others over half the economic worth of their labours. Few farmers had reserves to see them through illness, drought or economic depression - with the result that money lenders flourished and expropriation of peasant lands in favour of wealthy absentee landlords was a common occurence.

Discontent was rife among the peasantry. The Jewish historian, Josephus, tells us that there were repeated uprisings against the authorities by disaffected peasants. Roman occupation authorities found

47

it necessary to suppress several bands of rebellious Jews which were led sometimes by social bandits and sometimes by self-styled 'prophets' or 'messiahs'. But the most graphic evidence of the troubled state of the land became evident in the year 66, when almost all of the Jewish population rose up in arms against the Roman occupation. The Roman-Jewish War lasted four years, with three more for mopping up operations. There was enormous loss of life and destruction of property. By the year 70, the city of Jerusalem was in ruins and the temple destroyed.

This was the world in which Jesus of Nazareth did his work of teaching and healing. As we read the gospels today we must place them in this turbulent time, against the background of the gross injustices and profound afflictions experienced by the common people within the daily stress and struggle of village life.

Jesus was not neutral in the economic, social and religious conflicts of his day. He sought by word and deed to create self-worth and self-respect among the lower classes, encouraging them to resist the predations of a social and economic order which undermined the quality of their lives. Unfortunately, many commentators on Jesus' work have focused only on his compassionate concern for individuals. This good work in itself, however, does not explain the hostility to Jesus by the religious and political authorities. These powerful elite classes would not have been disturbed if Jesus had only been a comforter of the downtrodden. Charitable deeds to persons in need do not in themselves rock any boats. No: the heart of Jesus' work, the cutting edge of his public actions, must be found elsewhere - and that 'elsewhere' is in words and deeds which challenged a public order victimizing the large majority of Jews. To denounce the religious purity code which labelled most people 'sinners'; to condemn the discriminatory valuation of people by the social code of honour and shame; to attack the temple establishment which was the centre for the organization of economic exploitation - these actions caused Jesus, the prophet from Nazareth, to be seen as a dangerous man.

Mark, early in his gospel and after recording some of Jesus' public works of teaching and healing, editorializes, "The Pharisees went out and immediately conspired with the Herodians against him, how to destroy him." (3:6) As we read this we need to remember that denigration of the Pharisees present in the four gospels is considered by scholars to be an historical anachronism. The low opinion of the Pharisees in Christian circles surfaced decades after the time of Jesus as a result of antagonism in certain locales between the newly emerging Jesus Movement and Jewish synagogues. This was the time in which the gospels were being composed. By contrast, the Pharisaic Party of Jesus' day would not have been a decisive factor in the opposition to his work. They taught and strictly observed the ritual demands of the Law of Moses, and they scorned Jews who failed to do so. But their discomfort with Jesus' neglect of the law would not have made them his mortal foes.

In our reading of the gospels we must make a clear distinction between Pharisees, on the one hand, and Sadducees and Herodians on the other. Both of the latter groups collaborated with the Roman authorities in oppressing the lower classes and in suppressing peasant discontent. Sadducees, who had charge of the Jerusalem temple, were a wealthy priesthood who feared that Jesus' words and deeds had revolutionary implications for that society. The political party of the Herodians feared Jesus might have seditious intentions. It is not likely that the Pharisees were part of the active Sadducean-Herodian conspiracy to have Jesus destroyed.

Much of the peasantry, on the other hand, heard and responded enthusiastically to Jesus. The heavily-exploited rural classes provided the labour upon which the productive wealth of the land depended - but a mood of rebellion was widespread among them. Given this unstable social situation, anyone who furthered the spiritual and social emancipation of the peasantry was suspected by the elite classes of revolutionary intent. Watching Jesus among the people, the Roman authorities together with their Jewish allies decided they could not tolerate yet one more itinerant preacher, healer and prophet who challenged the established order. They conspired to have Jesus put to death.

J.D. Crossan observes:

> Even if we can never know for sure what immediate
> cause resulted in crucifixion, Jesus' incarnated

enactment of the Kingdom of God as a program of resistance . . . must eventually have resulted in a fatal collision with official authority. It was only a matter of at what time and in what place. It was only a matter of whether his general attitude or some specific incident would lead finally to that inevitable martyrdom. Further, it is not necessary to make monsters of either Caiaphas or Pilate to understand their collaborative action against him. If you announce a Kingdom of God, it could easily be taken as claiming that you yourself are its king and, although neither Jewish nor Roman authorities saw Jesus as a military danger, since they did not round up his followers, they clearly saw him as a social one, since they did not execute him privately.

("Excavating Jesus", 218)

Faced with growing opposition, Jesus was forced to make a choice. He could have retired quietly from the scene, aware that continuing his public work would bring him to certain death. Each of the gospels portrays him struggling with this decision and each shows his determination to stay the course. In the end he was true to his own words, "No one who puts a hand to the plow and looks back is fit for the kingdom of God" (Lk 9:62).

The crucifixion of Jesus was the direct result of religious, social and economic conflict in that society, conflict which is now well documented and understood by historians. Jesus' words and actions were carefully formed responses to that conflict, his way of giving obedience to God. He was committed to the practice of justice and compassion in human relationships. He unmasked the arrogant pretensions and self-serving actions of the ruling classes; he challenged the social code of honour and shame; he criticized traditional ritual purity laws; he invited poor people to build communities in which mutual guidance, support and care would replace individualistic and competitive struggle for survival. And he treated people of all social classes with attention and respect. All of this he embraced as his assignment under Yahweh, fully aware of the risks to himself.

Jesus was put to death by the authorities because, upon leaving Nazareth and after receiving baptism from John, he took up the work of a prophet, healer and teacher. In his person and by his actions he proclaimed that the Reign of God had arrived because he was now putting into practice God's plan for the transformation of human relationships. In the eyes of the authorities, both Roman and Jewish, both occupying power and temple establishment, he was first seen as suspect, later as dangerous, and finally as seditious. He was viewed as an enemy to the established social order who must be removed. The violent death of Jesus followed inevitably from the manner in which he conducted his public life.

If we are to comprehend the depths of Jesus' personal struggle as he participated in these critical times of the Jewish people, we must understand that in everything he did there was an interior cost. Given the external circumstances of his life, which largely determined the shape of his public ministry, his spiritual commitment to the righteous Reign of God was certain to bring him profound inner struggle and sorrow. When did Jesus' crucifixion really begin? When did the deep sorrows of his life start? What was the cost he paid daily within himself for the mounting suspicion and rejection he endured as a result of his public actions? As we survey the gospels' accounts of increasing opposition to Jesus by the authorities, we must speak of an 'interior cross' which he endured in his heart, a cross of which the wood of Calvary was the ultimate and inevitable external manifestation.

Matthew 23:37 pictures Jesus looking over the holy city with love and grief: "Jerusalem, Jerusalem, the city that kills the prophets and stones those who are sent to it! How often I have desired to gather your children together as a hen gathers her brood under her wings, and you were not willing!" Luke 19: 41-42 speaks of the same event: "As he came near and saw the city, he wept over it, saying, 'If you, even you, had only recognized on this day the things that make for peace! But now they are hidden from your eyes.'" Both evangelists portray profound anguish within the Master because of his beloved people. In this cry from the heart, Jesus experiences the same agony which the psalmist of old heard within the heart of his God:

> I am the Lord your God,
> who brought you up out of the land of Egypt.

Open your mouth wide and I will fill it.
But my people did not listen to my voice;
    Israel would not submit to me.
So I gave them over to their stubborn hearts,
    to follow their own counsels.
O that my people would walk in my ways!

(Ps 81:10-13)

There is a strong suggestion in the gospels that Jesus repeatedly had experiences in his public ministry which pierced his soul. We may imagine him walking the land with knowing eyes and a vulnerable heart. He was moved by the injustices inflicted upon and the suffering endured by the peasantry; his anguish and dismay mounted as he observed the spiritual blindness and resistance to his message by Sadducee and Herodian. And to all of this he returned a love of incalculable generosity. In him we see both God's eternal sorrow for human sin and God's creative purpose to heal and transform human hearts.

There is a story told about Peter Abelard, perhaps apocryphal but nevertheless revealing. Abelard was a monk of the medieval Church noted for his great learning and wonderful teaching abilities but who was condemned as a heretic by the rigid and powerful orthodoxy of those times. It is said that one day he and a student were strolling through a wood, deeply engrossed in a conversation about the meaning of the cross of Jesus. The student was having difficulty understanding Abelard's instruction. Then they happened upon a large tree trunk which had fallen across the path and which a thoughtful forester had cut through in order that travellers could continue without having to scramble over the fallen tree. Pointing to the separated trunk, Abelard asked the young man, "Where do the rings in the wood of the tree begin and where do they end?" The young man replied, "They go to the roots of the tree far to the left and continue to the topmost branches far to the right." "And yet", said Abelard, "they are only visible to us here, at the cut. The cross of Jesus is like this cut. In that cross we are shown the heart of God broken for the sin of humanity, but like the rings of the tree that divine sorrow extends as far back as history begins and will continue until the End Time."

52

This story speaks of the interior meaning of the death of Jesus. He reflected within himself the broken heart of God. He accepted a path of lowliness, rejection, suffering and violent death because that kind of path becomes inevitable for any resolute apostle of love in a world rebelling against love. This was Jesus' choice. And there have always been women and men who have made that choice because of their decision to follow the way of love. They too have sometimes met with violent death as a result. One thinks of Christian martyrs throughout the centuries, and more recently of the murdered family of Rigoberta Menchu of Guatemala, recipient of a Nobel Peace prize, and of the slain Archbishop Oscar Romero of El Salvador. When evil rises up to deny love, sometimes there is a crucifixion.

THE RESURRECTION EXPERIENCE

The Gospel of John, Chapters 20 and 21, gives us several resurrection stories. The first tells of Mary Magdalene going to the tomb of Jesus on the third day after his crucifixion. Weeping, she sees angels there who ask why she weeps:

> She said to them, "They have taken away my Lord, and I do not know where they have laid him." When she had said this, she turned around and saw Jesus standing there, but she did not know that it was Jesus. Jesus said to her, "Woman, why are you weeping? Whom are you looking for?" Supposing him to be the gardener, she said to him, "Sir, if you have carried him away, tell me where you have laid him, and I will take him away." Jesus said to her, "Mary!" She turned and said to him in Hebrew, "Rabbouni!" (which means Teacher).
>
> (John 20:13-17)

The Gospel of Luke devotes Chapter 24 to a lengthy account of two men walking from Jerusalem to Emmaus, on that same third day. The risen Jesus joins them, incognito:

> Then beginning with Moses and all the prophets, he interpreted to them the things concerning himself in all the scriptures. As they came near the village to which they were going, he walked ahead as if he were going on. But they urged him strongly, saying, "Stay with us, because it is almost evening and the day is now nearly

over." So he went in to stay with them. When he was at the table with them, he took bread, blessed and broke it, and gave it to them. Then their eyes were opened, and they recognized him; and he vanished out of their sight.

(Luke 24:27-31)

The importance of these stories resides in the beautiful, dramatic and arresting manner in which they point to human experience of the crucified Jesus as living, as being present after his death to persons who had earlier responded joyfully to the divine love he incarnated. It has been said that "Emmaus never happened; Emmaus is always happening". These gospel stories sprang from human/Divine encounter which is possible for believers anywhere, any time. The experience of being in the company of the Risen One has been happening throughout the ages. The Spirit of the Holy One who took Jesus through death to new life was the same Spirit who enabled the people in these stories to experience the Risen One among them. Encounters with the living Jesus are vivid, startling and unexpected; stories about such encounters usually report the experience of profound spiritual transformation in the human subjects. Such stories tell of experiences the depths of which ultimately defy literal representation. We are in the realm of mystery, of mythical speech, of sacred storytelling.

Claims by the earliest followers of Jesus that they knew him alive after death would not in themselves have surprised their contemporaries. Most Jews of Jesus' time believed in a resurrection of the just after death, and apparitions of dead people were commonly reported.

Almost throughout the Old Testament period it was held that the dead continue to exist in the underworld, a region of shadows, misery and futility . . . . The name for this region was Sheol (Hebrew), Hades (Greek), (English versions, usually, Hell). . . . But with the deepening sense of God's omnipresence there seem to have arisen protests against this exclusion of Jehovah from what was coming slowly to be recognized as a part of this universe.

By New Testament times belief in the resurrection of the dead was held by all Jews except the die-hard Sadducees. . . . The universality of the belief in the resurrection of the dead was due primarily to the growth

of the apocalyptic point of view. God must one day
vindicate and reward his faithful ones, who were suffering
such cruel persecutions at the hands of the Gentiles.

(A. Richardson,
"A Theological Word Book of the Bible",106)

The Jewish leaders would not have been scandalized by the followers of Jesus if they had merely declared their belief that, as a just man,
Jesus was resurrected by God after death. Something else troubled
Jewish and Roman authorities about the emerging Jesus movement;
something new and disturbing was present in the first Christians after
they had experienced the risen Jesus. Luke records episodes of this
kind in the Book of Acts (e.g. Chapters 3 & 4). These Christians were
possessed by a startled awareness and growing conviction that the risen
One in their midst was inviting and enabling them to take up a new and
radical manner of life, the kind of life he himself had incarnated among
them. The resurrection experience was not a new *gnosis*, a new wisdom;
on the contrary, it was a call to a new *praxis*, to a new ethic. It was this new
way of life which troubled imperial and religious authorities, and for
precisely the same reasons which had brought them to the point of
having Jesus crucified. This was the seed of social, economic and
spiritual revolution.

On one occasion during Jesus' public ministry, disciples of John the
Baptist had come asking if Jesus is "the one who is to come, or are we to
wait for another?".

And he answered them, "Go and tell John what you have
seen and heard: the blind receive their sight, the lame
walk, the lepers are cleansed, the deaf hear, the dead are
raised, the poor have good news brought to them."

(Lk 7:21-23; & para: Mt 11:3-6)

This message is echoed in Lk 4:18-19 and Mk 2:15-17, and all three
echo texts from the great Hebrew prophets of biblical times.

The new Christians of resurrection experience had a radical hope
which they brought to marginalized people, to those who were being
victimized in that socio-economic system. (This point is developed fully in
"The Message and the Kingdom", Horsely and Silberman.) They brought

a gospel of healing transformation to human relationships. They looked for a coming Reign of God in righteousness and peace.

Unfortunately, this hope and this promise present in the early Jesus Movement became submerged by the Jewish apocalyptic ethos of those times. Expectations that the Reign of God could begin to be realized among those people, at that time and in that place, were put on hold as increasing numbers of the earliest Christians looked for the Second Coming of the Lord to close the present age within their lifetimes .

During more than five centuries before the time of Jesus, the Jews had been developing expectations concerning a final ingathering of the nations and a salvation to be wrought by God for a persecuted and dispersed Israel. Many Jews believed that God would break into history and create a New Jerusalem, that they would be taken into an Age of Righteousness and Peace. The prophecies of a man we know only as Third Isaiah (c.530 BCE) resonated with these Jewish yearnings to be delivered from suffering experienced under oppressive imperial domination:

> Violence shall no more be heard in your land,
>> devastation and destruction within your borders;
>> you shall call your walls Salvation and your gates Praise.
> Strangers shall stand and feed your flocks,
>> foreigners shall till your land and dress your vines;
> but you shall be called priests of the Lord,
>> you shall be named ministers of our God;
> you shall enjoy the wealth of the nations,
>> and in their riches you shall glory.
>> (Isaiah 60:18, 61:5-6)

In the centuries both before and after this oracle, the Jews were oppressed by a series of imperial conquests. Assyria and Babylon brought devastation and exile but, in contrast, the suzerainty of the Persians was relatively benign. However, invasion by the Greeks in 335 BCE and by the Romans in 63 BCE brought nothing but grief for the majority of Jews. Palestine was looted for its agricultural wealth, the Hebrew religion suffered frequent humiliation, and foreign governors placed in the land were often ruthless in their policies.

It was during these hard times that the prophecies of Isaiah and other

Jewish sages gave birth to full-blown apocalyptic expectations, to hopes and revelations about a violent breaking into history of the End Time. Apocalyptic writing used mystical symbols to suggest a time, soon to come, when Yahweh would overcome Israel's enemies and bring the Chosen People into an age of social and economic bliss (as, for example, in the Book of Daniel, and in the Jewish sect known as Essenes). The thrust of apocalyptic faith was to encourage people whose lives were desperately difficult to believe that their sufferings would not last forever. God would come to deliver them, just as God had delivered their ancestors from slavery in Egypt many centuries earlier.

After Jesus' death and resurrection, Christian hope became infected with this apocalyptic virus, and with unfortunate results. The daily life and witness of the early Christians became penetrated by apocalyptic expectations. They looked for Jesus to come soon, to close the present evil age. Jesus' own commitment to building the Reign of God in justice, compassion and peace *within history* became replaced by pious yearnings for his Second Coming in a cataclysmic *end to history*. Easter Day seems at first to have echoed the Passover celebration of the historic Exodus from oppression and entry into freedom; early chapters of the "Acts of the Apostles" tell of community sharing of goods and works of healing. But eventually Easter Day became a celebration of the promise of eternal life in an imminent Day of Judgment, an expectation of eternal life for 'good' people but not for 'bad' people. The resurrection experience lost much of its true meaning.

An adequate reading of the resurrection experience proclaims it as an empowering for personal and social transformation and a call to serve the work of justice, compassion and peace in the world. This reading affirms Jesus as a prophet in Galilee, a servant of the people, a sign of God's presence, dedicated to the coming Reign of God in righteousness and peace. This reading declares Jesus was raised from death into glory to be first born and pre-eminent among many sisters and brothers who have laboured and continue to labour for the Reign of God which appears among us here and there in the present time. Resurrection life rejoices in gifts of the Spirit which enable us to be servants and signs of Sacred Presence in the daily affairs of life.

57

Ched Myers, in his commentary on the Gospel of Mark, "Binding the Strong Man" (401), suggests that this gospel

> ... ends with a challenge to the reader in the form of an unresolved question. Will we "flee" or will we "follow"? This cannot be resolved in the narrative moment, only in the historical moment of the reader. Whether or not we actually "see" Jesus again depends upon whether the disciples/readers renew their commitment to the journey. It is at this point that we should recall the mysterious words of 9:10: "And they held fast to his word, but discussed among themselves 'What is the meaning of resurrection from the dead?'" Here at the end of the story we find ourselves in exactly the same position. We do not entirely understand what "resurrection" means, but if we have understood the story, we should be "holding fast" to what we do know: that Jesus still goes before us, summoning us to the way of the cross. And that is the hardest ending of all: not tragedy, not victory, but an unending challenge to follow anew. Because that means we must respond.

Bohoeffer's famous question will always be with us:

"Who is Jesus for us today?"

Over many years I have addressed that question by writing prayers for personal use. Each prayer has begun with general notions and feelings and phrases, duly recorded in my "little book of words"; and with time and continuing revisions they resolve themselves into a prayer-poem. These I use to bring me before Jesus, and Jesus before me. I never know when a prayer will become inadequate; but when it does, I begin the search for the next one. It is a gentle process of discovering a relationship.

> Jesus of Nazareth, prophet in Galilee,
>   radiant with the Mystery of Lowliness:
>   you were a wise servant or your people,
>   you revealed the beautiful Way of the Reign of God.
> Though powerful enemies rejected and killed you.
>   Holy Love in you prevailed;
>   your truth and love abide among us.
> Beloved Teacher and Friend,
>   we desire to live this day as your disciples,
>   to be open to gifts of the Spirit
>   which come to those who follow your Way,
>   that as people of compassion, justice and peace
>   we also may be signs of God's presence in the world.

> To put it in Christian terms, the affirmation of suffering [by the one who suffers] is part of the great 'yes' to life as a whole. . . . an attempt to see life as a whole as meaningful and to shape it as happiness. It is an eternal affirmation of temporal reality. The God who is the lover of life does not desire the suffering of people, not even as a pedagogical device, but instead their happiness
>
> (Dorothy Soelle, "Suffering", 108)

The Story told in each of the four gospels of the New Testament develops through a narration of the public ministry of Jesus of Nazareth, lasting perhaps one and a half years, before reaching a closing climax. We are told of his arrest, of judicial trials and sentencing, and finally of his death on a cross. This instrument of public disgrace, torture and death was well known to Jews of that time; the Romans used it to great effect whenever they sought to control subject peoples. The section of each gospel which records these events is generally termed 'the passion narrative'.

A remarkable feature of all four passion narratives is that, though Jesus himself is ostensibly on trial, the evangelists portray him as placing his accusers on trial (Mt 26-27, Mk 14-15, Lk 22-23, Jn 18-19). It seems impossible to read the passion narratives and remain unmoved by the quiet and self-composed way in which Jesus responds to every insult and vindictive assault. As the events unfold, his innocence is made apparent and the ignorance and malice of his enemies revealed. This is not surprising. The evangelists believed not only in Jesus' innocence but also in his God-given power to overcome the animosity of his accusers with deliberate goodwill and generosity. Each evangelist told his story so that we the readers will wonder about this man and perhaps pause in the hastening of our own lives to ask what he may mean to us.

But the evangelists also leave us with unanswered questions. Was something happening in Jesus' passion which has enduring significance for all time? Was there something present in how he died which we must notice if we are to grasp the full meaning of how he lived?

Christians throughout the ages have interpreted Jesus' manner of death as revealing his compassion for all people - even for those who disregard God's will for their lives. Luke emphasized this interpretation when he reported Jesus' words from the cross, "Father, forgive them; for they do not know what they are doing". More than a few people have known personal transformation as they recognized and accepted for themselves the loving action of God for humanity manifest in Jesus' death. This experience is echoed throughout the New Testament. And, as we have already seen, a careful reading of the Hebrew Scriptures reveals testimony to a divine compassion and forgiveness which would bring eventual salvation to all nations. But still the question lingers, "If for a righteous man one would hardly die, why then for the unrighteous?"

An unusual book which crossed my path some years ago may help to illuminate this question. In "The Temple of God's Wounds" by Will Quinlan, the author tells of making a retreat where "the Temple Community is equally indifferent to being known or unknown. God brings to it those who need it, and there is anxiety neither to recruit nor to withhold membership. . . . I have however taken the precaution of giving no indication of the whereabouts of the Temple." The reader soon realizes that the author has chosen to share profound experiences in his own life journey under the image of a retreat made in a symbolic setting.

Quinlan's imagined retreat consists of seven days, each day being given to meditation upon one of seven pictures placed around the circumference of the Temple of God's Wounds. The first picture shows Jesus of Nazareth being crucified, and the author describes his response to what he sees:

> The Christ, crowned with thorns, lay stretched upon the cross. His hands were already fixed. A man crouched above him, with feet astride and buttocks resting on the waist of the Christ, and arms wielding a heavy hammer with which he was driving home the nail which pierced the two feet. . . . The poise of the hammering figure suggested the rhythm of long practice, and the impersonality of habitual craftsmanship. It drew my attention at first more fully than the prostrate one. How unconcerned it looked; how callously intent upon its task. As the hammer was a tool in his hands, so was this man a tool to those whose minds had conceived, and whose lips had ordered, this outrage. The plotting of the High Priests; the betrayal in the Garden; the flight of the

twelve; the denial of their chief; the trial with its shifts and illegalities; the arraignment before the Roman Governor, his judicial acquittal, and stratagems to avoid an unjust condemnation; the rejection by the people; the mockery of Herod; the crowning with thorns; the scourging; the sending forth on the sorrowful way to this place of execution: all were behind the swing of that uplifted arm.

As I watched the rhythm of that hammer, my grief was deep and bitter. Every crime against the helpless and innocent was an added blow upon that nail. My own folk were striking many such blows, now, in the very country and place of my dwelling.

Yet half-consciously I knew that still there remained a feeble barrier against a further conviction which carried horror with it. . . . I knew with complete conviction that as my own folk had proved to be, so was I myself.

(26-30)

The author has allowed his imagination free rein, working with and adding to images in the picture before him. In that dense, dark scene he perceives the sin of the world, the suffering of Jesus, and the depths of Jesus' love for humanity. Will Quinlan shares with his readers how, as he contemplated the crucifixion, his heart was moved by an inner contrition which changed his life.

That picture was the first of seven in the seven-sided Temple. As Quinlan progressed through the week and meditated on each of the pictures, he saw the wondrous light of God's love shining through Jesus to transform the darkness that Quinlan perceived in his society and in his own heart. He saw an active divine loving which can transform human life.

During his public ministry Jesus spoke parables in which he pointed to a quality of love which transforms life. We have already considered in detail one of these parables, about a father and two sons. In the parable, the father's anguish for his lost son had reached to the depths of his soul. In this kind of suffering, the afflicted person feels that what she or he is experiencing ought not to be happening. The alienation of son from father ought not to have happened. In this kind of suffering we feel that something has gone wrong in the natural order of things, some basic justice is being violated. Job, in the Hebrew writing of that name, resigned himself to the early catastrophes which overcame him even

61

though they inflicted unimaginable misery and pain. But there came a time when his pain deepened, it changed in character - and he cursed God. Now he was overwhelmed with his sufferings because there was no longer any discernible meaning in what was happening to him. He experienced a totally inexplicable violation of his being. The essence of suffering of that depth is that for the sufferer it has no explanation.

It is true that some people can endure such suffering for a time, gritting their teeth, forcing themselves to bear without complaint terrible bodily and mental agony in a spiritual void. But strength for that forbearance does not last forever: eventually one will curse life itself. "Would that I had never been born", cries Job. On the other hand, as soon as such suffering is infused with even the slimmest of meaning it loses the quality of dread. The struggle eases and we are less in the grip of spiritual death. Even though the physical and mental pain and spiritual suffering may persist, we are released from utter demoralization and can participate again in human society, and perhaps without debilitating bitterness.

When we can move from an inexplicable interior suffering which makes life not worth living to a kind of resignation which relieves anger and bitterness, we have experienced a change for the better. We have crossed some kind of threshold.

There is, however, a further threshold which suffering people can move through. Because of their own suffering they may become aware of how much suffering there is elsewhere in the world and then they pass from concern for self to concern for others. They become able to transcend their own suffering as they discover in themselves an urgent, compassionate love for other suffering people. This is what we see in the father of Jesus' parable; this is what we see in the crucified Jesus.

This holy, transforming love is dramatically evident in the crucifixion scenes of the passion narratives; though it is less obvious in the other gospel stories about Jesus, it is also present there. His life and his death form one seamless unity.

It is important to realize that Jesus of Nazareth did not choose suffering for himself, as though that were some kind of desirable and heroic achievement. As Dorothé Soelle says, suffering has no value in itself. Jesus entered into his suffering willingly because he made a decision to be an instrument of God's work of compassion and justice and, given the social and political conditions which confronted him, that choice meant accepting crucifixion. Because his choice was made with an 'amazing grace' of love for others, his dying on a cross continues to be transformative for humanity and has become a wondrous icon of the active divine loving pouring itself into creation. In these things there is indeed a mystery of lowliness.

> To be a Christian does not mean to be religious in a particular way, to cultivate some particular form of asceticism (as a sinner, as a penitent or a saint), but to be [human]. It is not some religious act which makes a Christian what he is, but participation in the suffering of God in the life of the world.
>
> (Dietrich Bonhoeffer,
> "Letters and Papers from Prison", July 18/44)

In the passion and cross of Jesus of Nazareth we see the foundational paradigm of this "participation in the suffering of God in the life of the world". Indeed Jesus is for the Christian the absolute statement of this kind of loving. We say: "God was in Christ Jesus". In him - in all his loving, as in his dying - the eternal generosity of the active divine loving can be seen, recognized and accepted by us for the transforming of our lives.

But sadly, it is this very seeing, recognizing and accepting which seem so often to elude us. We sense that Love desires to accomplish our inner transformation. But even as we feel the invitation, the extent and significance of the change ahead is unknown to us and this generates fear, resistance and refusal. The possibility of offering to Love a responding trust seems beyond our strength. What, then, can bring us to that "humble and contrite heart" of which the psalmist sings, which opens the human heart to the Divine? When the initiative of the active divine loving is being felt, where do we find the will to say 'yes'?

Once again we are in the realm of spiritual reality, of sublime mystery, and of sacred story. If we are to appreciate and respond to the reach of God's active loving for us, we need to hear stories which others have to tell about that loving. While Love which shines from the cross is whole

63

and pure, there are unnumbered significant manifestations of transforming love present in everyday human relationships. We need the support of believing communities which hear, remember, treasure and retell our sacred stories.

Some years ago I was told a story by a friend, a member of Alcoholics Anonymous, which illustrates this kind of experience. It tells of a Christian pastor who had relinquished parish work to become a counsellor to alcoholics. A certain man who came often to see the pastor was caught in the destructive pattern of going 'dry' for a time and then returning to drink. One day, further than ever into the abuse of alcohol, the man went again to see his pastor friend. As the troubled man talked, tears came to the listener's eyes, tears from the heart - but no words of counsel were offered. These were not tears of pain or frustration; these were tears of loving identification with the other which flowed as the weeping man took upon himself the suffering of the other. The tears were 'of God', and they opened the way for transformation of the sick man. When he left that room, this man never used alcohol again. It was he who first told this story.

It is important not to hear this as a touching story about human friendship. Present between those two men was an Exchange of Love: an act of redemptive suffering on the part of one and a gift of transformation for the other. The active agent for both men was the Spirit.

In meditating on the crucifixion of Jesus, many people have found there a similar power for personal transformation.

A second story concerns an elderly lady in whose house I had set up a small woodworking area while I was a university student. She was a severe diabetic and one day she postponed taking her insulin and went instead to the basement for a jar of preserves. This was a bad mistake because she blacked out and fell on the basement floor, breaking her pelvis.

In those days, the Montreal General Hospital on Lagauchetiere Street had horseshoe-shaped wards, each holding about twenty-five beds. When I went to visit my friend, I found the space for her bed empty. I asked at the desk for her whereabouts and a nurse pointed me to the far

64

end of the ward where several patients were gathered around a bed standing out in an open area. The nurse said, "Mrs. Rigby is a ray of sunshine. The other patients go to her to get cheered up."

A couple of years later, when I had moved from Montreal, I received a Christmas letter from Mrs. Rigby saying that a further injury had meant the amputation of a leg, but that she was so grateful to God for all the blessings of that year. I remember marvelling at her ability to make her times of suffering into occasions for others to be blessed.

A central truth of the crucifixion story is present in each of these contemporary stories, and in uncounted other such stories down through the centuries.

The transformation needed in human life is not only personal but social. The brokenness and sinfulness of the human species is everywhere evident in the disorder which afflicts social, economic and political life. Isaiah of Jerusalem saw this in his temple vision; Peter Abelard spoke of it when he called attention to the sorrow in the Heart of God throughout the millenia of human history; Will Quinlan felt it deeply as he meditated upon the crucifixion scene. In our world there are unnumbered instances of radical social injustice waiting for the creative response of the work of justice which springs from love for others. Two can serve here as illustrative.

The first is the international garment industry. In Mexico, Central America, South-East Asia and metropolitan cities of the world there are workers, chiefly young women, whose working conditions are dangerous and whose wages are subsistence level or less. These are the notorious 'sweat shops' which produce most of the world's clothing and footwear. These are places of 'structural evil' because we are beyond interpersonal acts of sin and are faced with economic systems which in their impersonal operation bring oppression and death to their victims. The source of the evil lies in patterns of human degradation which are, at least for now, tolerated by governments and peoples.

The second example is the armaments industry. Again we are beyond personal immorality and are confronted by structural evil. The sheer waste of valuable natural resources, the monumental financial costs (approaching one trillion dollars annually for the world), and the continuing devastation of persons, property and the environment together constitute one of the most acute contemporary forms of structural sin. Any work of transformation in this arena and others of similar complexity must address pressing questions of social, political and economic life.

In what form, then, do we see active divine loving addressing and seeking to transform such extensive expressions of human social sin and structural evil? We see it in the wise, urgent and self-sacrificing compassionate actions of countless people who seek to dismantle systemic injustice and to build new social and economic systems founded upon justice and peace.

We have already noticed that one characteristic action of Jesus' public life was to call people into new and different relationships which would bring both personal and social transformation. In the early Jesus Movement there was evidence of a communal solidarity which sought to bring greater justice to their shared life as disciples of the Master. However, social compassion and social justice have often been tragically absent from the church and denied by the actions of confessing Christians. It is gratifying, then, to find a commitment to social compassion and social justice at the heart of contemporary black, liberation, feminist and ecological theologies. It is to be found also within contemporary communities of all kinds which seek to change unjust social relations within their own communal life. Without the passion for social transformation, without our commitment to the well-being of the entire social order, the goal of wholeness in personal life will continue to elude us.

CHAPTER SUMMARY

When he was about thirty years old, Jesus of Nazareth went with crowds of Jewish villagers living in Roman Palestine to receive baptism by the prophet John in the Jordan River. That experience was life transforming for him.

We learn from the gospels that Jesus believed himself sent by his God to carry out public healing and teaching, to a work of drawing people into new and creative relationships with one another. As he travelled about, his commitment to the well-being of the common people was constantly demonstrated. His teaching about the generosity and compassion of God was built upon the best religious traditions of his people.

Jesus challenged both the discriminatory religious practices and the unjust social and political arrangements which victimized the peasantry. As a result, he endeared himself to the lower classes who flocked to him, but alienated the elite classes. His actions were seen by the authorities of the Roman occupation as potentially dangerous since there was a mood of rebelliousness among the peasantry which occasionally erupted in militant action. In addition, Jesus' association with the marginalized poor in table fellowship offended the upper classes. They considered such behaviour outrageous for a noted teacher. Very soon after his public life had begun, Herodians and Sadducees resolved to have him destroyed.

After a relatively short public life Jesus was arrested, tried and executed. Following crucifixion a number of his closest friends experienced the risen Jesus as present with them, empowering them, gifting them with new life in the Spirit. Jesus was not only a vivid memory; for those who loved him he was a continuing effective presence.

The crucified and risen Jesus is one of the most powerful examples we have of the kind of active loving which, through its own suffering, is able to reach the suffering of others with healing power, with new life. His example has also led many of his disciples throughout the centuries to challenge social and economic systems which destroy life, seeking by their actions of justice and compassion to assist societal transformation and renewal.

4

THE LURE OF POWER AND PRIVILEGE

The Synoptic tradition in Matthew, Mark and Luke presents Jesus of Nazareth as a man with a gospel. We see him being sent by God to announce the coming Reign of Righteousness and Peace, a reign which Jesus believed was being initiated in Galilee by his actions and his words. This is the Good News which even Jesus' enemies could not extinguish even though they caused him to be crucified.

A moment's reflection on the Christianity with which the world is most familiar, however, reveals something different. Jesus no longer has a gospel which he announces to the world. Jesus *is* the gospel which became entrusted to the church. In church tradition, the Good News is that Jesus died for us on the cross to save us from the consequences of sin. This is not the same as telling about Jesus' work to build the Kingdom of God, a work into which everyone is invited as co-workers.

In Jesus' work the focus is on the message. In the church's proclamation, the focus has been on the messenger. Though message and messenger are inextricably connected, which is emphasized has radical consequences for what we understand by Christian discipleship.

The change from Jesus' voice to the church's voice is not a trivial change. This is a profound shift in focus away from the Synoptic tradition and into the church tradition, a shift which found its central exposition and most powerful statement in the church's Doctrine of the Atonement. And this doctrine is today one of the most controversial elements in the teaching of the Christian church.

For at least 150 years, thoughtful Christians - not to mention non-Christians - have been questioning why a God who is presented in much of the Bible as the source of unconditional loving should need a human death to make possible the forgiveness of sin. From eminent contemporary Christian scholars we read comments like the following:

> If we reject and disobey the Creator, but then truly repent, why should God not simply accept our repentance as genuine, instead of continuing to insist on some impossible punishment or price for our sin?

The notion that God's only son came to this planet to offer his life as a sacrifice for the sins of the world, and that God could not forgive us without that having happened, and that we are saved by believing this story, is simply incredible.

(Marcus Borg:
"Meeting Jesus Again for the First Time", 131)

Along with other forms of political and liberation theology, feminist theology repudiates an interpretation of the death of Jesus as required by God in repayment for sin. Such a view today is virtually inseparable from an underlying image of God as an angry, bloodthirsty, violent and sadistic father. . .

(Elizabeth A. Johnson: "She Who Is", 158)

The notion of atoning sacrifice does not express the [early] Jesus movement's understanding and experience of God but is a later interpretation of the violent death of Jesus in cultic terms. The God of Jesus is not a God who demands atonement and whose wrath needs to be placated by human sacrifice or ritual.

(Elizabeth Schussler Fiorenza, "In Memory of Her", 130)

If [a] sense of the sacred character of the natural world as our primary revelation of the divine is our first need, our second need is to diminish our emphasis on redemption experience in favour of a greater emphasis on creation processes.

(Thomas Berry, "The Dream of the Earth", 81)

And in a satirical tone the same dissent is found in a popular folk song:

> Jesus died to save us from sin,
> Glory to God - we're goin' to need him again!

The felt need for atonement between human beings and the Eternal One comes directly from an image of God as omnipotent, righteous, and wrathful against human sin. In this view, the separation of humankind from God is the result of the utter incompatibility of sinful humanity and divine holiness. In order to be free to forgive human sin and to bring about an at-one-ment with humanity, this God is believed to require 'restitution', 'payment', 'propitiation' - all three words appear in the lexicon of atonement theology. Ancient Israel addressed the felt need for atonement through a complex sacrificial system which included the annual ritual of the Day of Atonement. The Christian church affirmed a universal atonement through the willing death on a cross of Jesus the God-Man. Both of these responses are rooted in a common image of God.

As we have seen already, however, there is a second opinion in the Hebrew Scriptures about the nature of God and of God's relationship to humankind. Jesus of Nazareth himself chose that second opinion when he taught about God as compassionate and lived that compassion in his own life. But because the church chose a different theological path - a path which it still follows in its doctrine of the Atonement - we must ask why this happened, what resulted from that choice, and why this doctrine must now be abandoned.

THE LAMB OF GOD

In the Fourth Gospel, John 1:29, John the Baptist is reported as saying of Jesus, "Here is the Lamb of God who takes away the sin of the world". This image of Jesus had its origins in two key elements of the faith and ritual of the ancient Hebrews. The first element came from the annual Passover commemoration of the foundational event of Israel's Grand Narrative: the escape from slavery in Egypt and the journey to another and good land. The second element came from the cultic ritual of the annual Day of Atonement.

The central action in the Passover festival was the killing and eating of a lamb. How this Passover festival entered Israel's history is sketched by F.J. Taylor in "A Theological Word Book of the Bible" (A. Richardson, ed.,163):

> It is generally believed that [the Passover] goes back far beyond the time of Moses, and in this remote origin consisted of two spring festivals, pastoral and agricultural, merged into one in historical times. The agricultural feast of unleavened bread and bitter herbs was combined with the primitive nomadic feast of the firstborn of the flock sacrificed at the same vernal season. . . . In the annual Passover festival the lamb had a commemorative

function. The ritual killing and eating of a lamb was the central symbolic action which reaffirmed and celebrated the covenant relationship between the ancient Hebrews and their God. . . . The slain lamb of Passover symbolically pointed to God's historic act of liberation.

The second element in the Christian image of Jesus as the atoning Lamb of God was drawn from the Hebrew ritual of atonement. The origins of the notion of atonement lie in the mists of ancient time, but its adaptation to Israel is associated with the time of Moses and his belief that God required the construction of a "Tent of Meeting". In this tent, among several other sacred objects, were two altars. One was for the burning of incense and the other for the burning of sacrifices. The Tent of Meeting was superseded centuries later by the building of a temple in Jerusalem. By this time there was a well-established priesthood, the beginnings of a detailed code telling why and how sacrifices were to be offered, and at least the core of a ritual for the annual Day of Atonement.

> Once a year the high priest entered the Holy of Holies to cleanse it of the defilement caused by sins. That occurred on the Day of Atonement, Yom Kippur, the holiest day of the Jewish year. It was necessary to purge God's dwelling of the defilement caused by the sin of the people because eventually the buildup of defilement would make it impossible for God to remain there. . . . [On the Day of Atonement] the high priest took a bull with which to make atonement for himself. He also took two goats, one of which was a "scape-goat". The guilt of the people would be placed upon the scape-goat and it would be driven into the desert. The other goat would make atonement for the sins of the people.
> (F.J. Murphy, "The Religious World of Jesus", 85-6)

There were, then, two Hebrew rituals which contributed to the Christian notion of a Lamb of God "who takes away the sin of the world". The ritual of the Passover lamb recalled an historic deliverance from slavery and into freedom, and the ritual of the scape-goat symbolized the annual removal of the nation's guilt before God due to its accumulated ritual impurity. However, as F.J. Taylor (ibid,164) points out, in the New Testament "Letter to the Hebrews", "the ritual of the day of Atonement, and not of the Passover, is used to interpret the death of Christ". That is,

71

the death of the Christ became primarily associated with deliverance from sin and the gift of eternal life, and not with the deliverance into the freedom of new life in the here and now.

By the time the "Letter to the Hebrews" was written, late in the first century or early in the second, Christian teaching about Jesus' death was emphasizing the need for atonement from sin and had exchanged the symbol of the scapegoat for the symbol of a lamb. The church's Lamb of God became, in Christian teaching, the agent who brought humanity the forgiveness of sin. (The ritual goat was out of a job!) In the process of this development, the Lamb imagery had lost almost all of its Jewish reference to Israel's experience of deliverance from slavery and entrance into new life.

The church changed the meaning of the lamb image from one of historic deliverance out of misery and injustice (Passover) to the notion of a payment to God to deliver humanity from divine wrath against sin and guilt (Atonement).

This shift in imagery - the alteration of traditional Hebrew symbolism by the early church - proved to be profoundly significant for the future of the church. By disconnecting the lamb image from its Hebrew context in Passover, the Christian church lost an interpretation of Jesus of Nazareth within the Exodus tradition. Mainstream Christian teaching failed to understand that Jesus of Nazareth acted in history for humanity's continuing exodus from social, economic and political injustice. The theme of communal deliverance from oppression and the gift of new life was suppressed and the theme of individual salvation from sin was given prominence.

It is noteworthy, however, that with the rise in recent decades of various liberation theologies, many Christians are naming Jesus as God's agent to establish a reign of justice and peace. These theologies interpret him as the fulfilment of the ancient Passover promise.

Unfortunately, the early church's teaching about Jesus as the Lamb of God, the one who by his death mediates divine forgiveness, implicitly denies the Hebrew vision of God as infinitely compassionate and freely forgiving. The reasons for this development in Christian theology are not clear - we have no records to show us how it happened. But it is clear that the image of Jesus as the Lamb of God "who takes away the sin of the world" gradually expanded and became inflated in church teaching, liturgy and personal devotions. There was a continual deepening of Christian theology and piety around this image, together with the elevation of Jesus to eternal glory. Soon he became the Christ of God, Saviour of the World, pre-existent Son of the Father and 'God of God'. Eventually he became Pantocrator - Creator of all things, transcending the created order, to be worshipped as the Eternal Word of God. In the doctrine of Jesus of Nazareth as the Lamb of God, a foundation was being laid for the subsequent universal pretensions of the Christian religion and of the Christian church.

A MYSTERY OF LOWLINESS

The three Synoptic Gospels - Matthew, Mark and Luke - do not portray Jesus of Nazareth as the eternal and enthroned Lamb of God. They reveal in him a 'mystery of lowliness'. His natural and direct speech, his gentle strength, his firm but humble relations with other people, his open and generous response to women, his quiet dependence on an intimate relationship with his God - in these and other ways the evangelists present a lowliness in Jesus which is seen to be his chief characteristic.

The theme of lowliness is also frequent in Jesus' teaching. It appears dramatically in a short parable found in Luke l2:35-37. Luke gives the parable a specific context: Jesus is instructing his twelve closest friends in behaviour fitting for the Kingdom or Reign of God. He begins:

> Be dressed for action and have your lamps lit; and be like those who are waiting for their master to return from the wedding banquet, so that they may open the door for him as soon as he comes and knocks. Blessed are those slaves whom the master finds alert when he comes. . .

As readers, we might well anticipate what Jesus meant by the servants being "alert". They would have candles lit, food prepared, a marital bed ready, and be full of congratulations and joy. They would desire to serve the master in any way possible. But Jesus actually finishes his little parable in a different manner: "Truly I tell you, he will fasten his belt and have them sit down to eat, and he will come and serve them." This conclusion to the story turns what we expect upside down. The master deliberately and surprisingly takes the role and work of a servant. Jesus is using shock tactics to propose a revolutionary understanding of himself and of how position and authority are to be understood in the Reign of God.

Another example of shock tactics is found in John 13. We are told that, after sharing a meal with the Twelve, Jesus "got up from the table, took off his outer robe, and tied a towel around himself. Then he poured water into a basin and began to wash the disciples' feet and to wipe them with the towel that was tied around him." It is impossible to over-estimate the bewilderment that the Twelve experienced at that moment. Peter objected strenuously, "Lord, are you going to wash my feet?", to which Jesus replied, "Unless I wash you, you have no share with me." To Peter and the others, Jesus' actions seemed preposterous. The master was choosing to be the servant.

Sayings and actions of Jesus often had within them a call to lowliness for those who would be his disciples. The parable in Luke 14:7-11 is about a host who gives a marriage feast. Jesus used the story to recommend to his audience not to seek "a place of honour" at the feast, but rather "to take the lowest place". One of his best-known aphorisms affirmed that "the first shall be last and the last shall be first". Moving about Galilee, he preferred to be among those without social status. In the language of that day, he chose to be with those with 'shame' rather than to be with those with 'honour'. He readily accepted the company of persons who in that society were marginalized, who were classified as 'unclean' and publicly referred to as 'sinners'. And though the evangelists report that "he spoke as one with authority, and not as the scribes and pharisees", his transparent authority did not lead him to seek precedence over the villagers and simple rural folk among whom he moved - a remarkable authority indeed. And the common people heard him gladly. Once we begin to be attentive to Jesus in his lowliness, we notice it repeatedly in the Synoptic Gospels.

Occasionally Jesus showed exasperation when anyone responded to his words and deeds with acclamation of his person. He appears to have declined all efforts to give him a special status. It was natural enough for people to want to act this way toward him but it contradicted his own self-understanding. Nowhere in the accounts of the Synoptic Gospels does Jesus of Nazareth exalt himself. And at the end of his life, when he is on trial before the authorities, he is represented as almost entirely silent, quietly accepting an unjust fate.

Not everyone in that society was favourably impressed by the chosen lowliness of this man. From the earliest days of his public ministry we see Jesus confronting and being confronted by authorities who take strong exception to his words and deeds. He has powerful enemies who are angered by the ways in which he challenges the traditional purity code, by the ways he regularly violates the accepted social code of honour and shame. He seems to have little regard for such social and religious distinctions. In his exchanges with the 'important' people, the lowliness of Jesus is seen in the unpretentious courage and the determined single-mindedness with which he defends his association with 'unimportant' persons and groups.

Jesus is consistently shown as concerned for and compassionate to the lower classes. In reaching out to them in their need, he was implicitly questioning the religious, social, political and economic arrangements which supported the privilege and power of the ruling groups. To reach out in care and concern to the one class was to be a threat to the power of the other and for this action Jesus was ultimately put to death by the authorities. Early in his gospel (3:6), after a confrontation with members of the social elite, Mark reports, "The Pharisees went out and immediately conspired with the Herodians against him, how to destroy him." Jesus must have been a paradoxical figure to his enemies. Renouncing privileges for himself, he sought by word and deed to gain justice for others. His lowliness was as offensive to his foes as it was valued by those who believed in him.

Jesus' lowliness is a sacred mystery because it held, and still holds, a power capable of transforming those who recognize and honour it. That transformative power is integral to everything Christians have meant by the divine love present in Jesus of Nazareth. It is a compelling form of power, an unusual authority. We might well wonder what kind of humility

75

was able, in love, to challenge but not seek to compel a rich man to abandon his wealth and join a roving band of disciples (Mk 10:17-22). What kind of meekness, we ask, appeared in the temple creating mayhem among corrupt commercial dealers but seeking no personal glory (Mk 11:15)? What kind of presence in the "lowest place" was able to pronounce the powerful "woes" upon scribe and lawyer, Pharisee and Sadducee, but gave no suggestion of moral arrogance (Mt 23:13-33)? What was the astonishing humility which was capable of holding steadily to a campaign of both compassion and confrontation, doing the Truth of God even though this brought him to agonizing death upon a cross? Such a mystery of lowliness may well fill us with wonder and lead us to a new sense of Sacred Presence.

In emphasizing lowliness in Jesus and calling attention to its importance for Christian discipleship, women may consider this to be an ambiguous assertion. Feminist writers have pointed out that in patriarchal society, women experience what might be termed a kind of 'enforced lowliness', experienced through normative cultural codes of behaviour and direct male coercion. This lowliness is a condition of subjection and degradation and is for women an experience of bondage. It is essential, therefore, to underline that the lowliness we see in Jesus was chosen by him in response to the Spirit's leading. For Christians this choice has always been a significant dimension of his strength and not a sign of weakness.

THE LANGUAGE OF EXALTATION

In contrast to the witness of the Synoptic Gospels to Jesus as a mystery of lowliness, other parts of the new Jesus Movement took up the language of exaltation by which to speak of him. This development became explicit in the Doctrine of the Atonement. In the language of exaltation the church found the means to affirm Jesus as the Lamb of God, the divine Redeemer, the Risen and Ascended Lord of the church. A clear example of this development is found in the New Testament "Letter to the Church at Ephesus" which was probably written by a disciple of the Apostle Paul early in the second century CE. The writer uses the language of exaltation to speak of Jesus the Christ as fulfilling

God's purposes:

> The hope to which God has called you . . .[comes] according to the working of his great power. God put this power to work in Christ when he raised him from the dead and seated him at his right hand in the heavenly places, far above all rule and authority and power and dominion, and above every name that is named, not only in this age but also in the age to come. And he has put all things under his feet and has made him the head over all things for the church, which is his body, the fullness of him who fills all in all.
>
> (Ephes. 1:19-22)

It is difficult to imagine a more exalted state than this. In other letters of the New Testament and even more so in "The Revelation to John" we encounter a steady litany of praise and power ascribed to Jesus the Risen and Ascended Lord. He is not only pictured as exalted in his final victory, he is divinized in his origins:

> He is the image of the invisible God,
> the firstborn of all creation;
> for in him all things in heaven and on earth were created, things visible and invisible, whether thrones or dominations or rulers or powers - all things have been created through him and for him.
>
> (Col 1:15-16)

Exaltation of the Lamb of God is present in every writing in the New Testament except the first three gospels. The Fourth Gospel, the last to be written, is noticeably different from the other three in style and content. In particular, John's Jesus affirms divinity for himself: "Before Abraham was, I am." In all the other "I am" sayings peculiar to this gospel, the evangelist has Jesus make claims which would justify his exaltation: "I am the Way, the Truth, and the Life", "I am the resurrection and the life", "I am the Light of the world", "I am the good shepherd", "I am living water", "I am the bread of life." This imagery is entirely consistent with the development of the language of exaltation about Jesus which had already emerged elsewhere in the early church. This imagery reflects the same theological discourse in which Jesus was pronounced "Lamb of God", but it was not present in the earliest layers of the Jesus tradition. Elizabeth Schussler Fiorenza comments:

> While the earliest Jesus traditions eschew any understanding of the ministry and death of Jesus in cultic terms as atonement for sins, it was precisely this interpretation which soon took root in some segments of the early Christian movement.
>
> ("In Memory of Her", 130)

It is very important, then, to notice the evolution of understanding, interpretation and symbolism which took place within the early Jesus Movement and which is reflected in the language of the New Testament. As Fiorenza observes, the dogma of Jesus' atoning death worked its way to the centre of Christian belief and constantly found expression "in cultic terms" within the early church's liturgies.

It is difficult, perhaps impossible, to know how much this was due to the teaching of the Apostle Paul and whether or not other key influences were also present. Paul's authentic letters, and others in the New Testament written under his influence, reflect this evolution of Christological understanding in the regions of Asia Minor and Greece. But judging by earlier written texts from Syria and Roman Palestine - sources for the Gospel of Mark and the gospel source known as "Q" - Lamb of God Christology was not current there in the earliest years.

We should note also that providing an atonement explanation for Jesus' death removed the need for church leaders to give due weight to the social, religious and political forces which had resulted in his judicial murder. Jealousy of Jesus within the religious establishment, suspicion of sedition by the Roman authorities, and other related social and economic forces, were in fact directly responsible for his crucifixion. Ignoring these factors made it easier for the church, using the language of exaltation, to interpret Jesus' death in mystical terms as a death required by God for the salvation of the world.

Christian teaching has never been clear about how Jesus' death achieved a universal salvation from sin, a salvation which could come in no other way. Paul the Apostle taught that by Jesus' death sinful humanity was reconciled to the righteous God:

> For while we were still weak, at the right time Christ died for the ungodly. . . . But the free gift is not like the trespass. For if the many died through the one man's

[Adam's] trespass, much more surely have the grace of God and the free gift in the grace of one man, Jesus Christ, abounded for the many.

(Romans 5: 6,15)

Other views of the atonement have differed from Paul. Early in the life of the church it was proposed that Jesus' death was a payment to Satan, a payment which secured our freedom from Satan's bondage. In the fourth century, Athanasius of Alexandria taught that through Jesus' death and resurrection all human flesh could be taken through a mystical death to sin and into a life of righteousness. In the eleventh century the British theologian Anselm taught that in his death Jesus the divine Son gave the eternal Father an act of perfect obedience. Anselm believed that this act made up for the moral debt to God which human sin had been accumulating since the days of Adam, and that the entire debt was cancelled by Jesus' obedient self-offering of "infinite worth". Other theories of the atonement have emerged since the l6th-century Reformation. Each of these depend heavily on personal faith in Jesus as the One whose substitute death as the Righteous One is said to free us from an eternal death we deserve for our sin.

No one theological explanation of Jesus as the atoning sacrifice has ever had general acceptance throughout Christendom. In spite of this, the church's proclamation of Jesus as the Lamb of God has remained the linchpin of her faith. But note: at the heart of all the variant explanations is an image of a God who cannot or will not forgive our sins without the intervention of Jesus' death. To this traditional affirmation we must respond firmly that though in former times this doctrine of God was widely believed, it is no longer credible. This teaching can have no place in the new Story which is emerging now.

It is a matter for profound regret, then, that the first Christians fastened on Israel's primitive image of a punitive God and neglected the prophetic vision of a compassionate God. The tension between these two images may well have been evident to Jesus of Nazareth as he grew into manhood in the Galilean village of Nazareth. However that may be, in the gospels of the New Testament we see clearly his personal testimony in word and deed to a compassionate God. Surely he would have been utterly dismayed and incredulous to hear himself named, "the Lamb of God who takes away the sins of the world".

DOMINANT TRADITION AND PROPHETIC IMPULSE

From the earliest days of the church there has been tension between the emphasis placed in official teaching on Jesus' power and exaltation, and a quieter but persistent witness to Jesus' lowliness and chosen role as a servant. These might be called the 'dominant tradition' and the 'prophetic impulse', two lasting legacies within the church's faith and life. Both have persisted from the beginning and both have clear distinguishing marks. Neither shows any sign of disappearing. The dominant tradition emphasizes the redemptive power of the Eternal and Sovereign Lord Jesus Christ, a Christology which became the heart of an orthodoxy which justifies and supports a magisterial ecclesiastical establishment. This tradition is evident today in the Sunday liturgies of Christian churches everywhere and in the customary teaching of the ordained clergy. In contrast, responses to a mystery of lowliness in Jesus have generated and sustained an alternative impulse of prophetic discipleship which has neither desired to find a place in the corridors of ecclesiastical power nor sought status in worldly affairs.

The dominant tradition refers to those tendencies and impulses which have sought temporal power, prestige and wealth for the church. This tradition exhibits a high degree of uncritical acceptance of the status quo in society. The prophetic impulse refers to voices which have protested when the church ceased to speak God's judgment against unrighteousness, both personal and social. Prophetic voices have attempted to bring believers to a greater faithfulness to biblical ethical ideals and to a deeper practice of compassion and justice. Moreover, a significant and frequent distinguishing mark of the prophetic impulse has been discomfort with aspects of the surrounding culture. It is, however, impossible to establish a hard line between the two tendencies and there seems always to have been Christians who see value in both.

Christians of both tendencies have adhered, generally speaking, to orthodox belief in the Atonement. However, they differ in the degree to which they use their advocacy of Salvation in Christ to seek status, wealth and public authority for the church. Reading church history it is clear that the dominant tradition has had the greater public presence. But reckoned in terms of enduring significance the reverse may be true. The human values present in the life of Jesus have been espoused for centuries by untold numbers of humble Christians as they have felt and responded to the spiritual authority of the prophetic impulse.

This impulse had its genesis within the little understood origins of ancient Israel (perhaps in the 10th century BCE) in the form of bands of 'nabi': roving ecstatics, soothsayers, and oracular speakers. From these early charismatics there developed both the court prophets who were in the paid service of the reigning monarchs, and authentic prophets of Yahweh like Micaiah and Elijah (9th century BCE) who, in opposition to court prophets, spoke to Israel their searching, controversial Word of the Lord. Prophets with scribal followers (secretaries who recorded some of their oracles) appeared in the golden age of prophecy during the last half of the 8th and the first half of the 6th centuries BCE. The core of this prophetic speech was a demand for righteousness in personal life and for justice in social relations.

There has been a succession of prophetic voices throughout the centuries calling the church to poverty of spirit, simplicity of life, compassionate ministry, and works of justice. These voices accented a devotion to and a following of the servant prophet of Nazareth, paying close attention to the gospels' testimony to the words and deeds of the historical Jesus. These voices represent the prophetic impulse within the life of the church.

Christians who have followed this latter path frequently found themselves in tension both with the dominant tradition of the Church and with contemporary social practice. A small sampling includes Anthony and his monks of the Egyptian desert (3rd and 4th centuries); Francis and Clare of Assisi (early 13th century) and their spiritual descendants in every age; monastic foundations in their early and reforming periods; religious Orders which have lived and served among the poor; Protestant communities from the Reformation which deliberately disavowed hierarchical organization and sought to express in their manner of living an egalitarian reading of the life of Jesus; radical Christian groups

81

organized to protest and ameliorate the social devastation of the early factory movement in Europe and North America; Dorothy Day and the Catholic Worker Movement; Jean Vanier and the L'Arche Community; the Iona Community in Scotland; and the Ecumenical Brotherhood of Taizé, France. There have been persons and communities in every age of the church who found their spiritual vision nurtured in Jesus' lowliness and servanthood.

The prophetic impulse in the church has for centuries sustained an awareness of the historical Jesus and his works of compassion. And in recent decades this impulse has been strengthened by biblical studies which have returned with new vigour to the 'search for the historical Jesus'. For many contemporary people, when adequate attention is given to Jesus of the gospels, to his words and his works, church teaching about eternal salvation through the Christ seems much less important.

TRIUMPHANT EXALTATION OF THE CHRIST AND ITS BITTER FRUIT

As the second century dawned on the Christian church, the language of exaltation had become ascendant. The Fourth Gospel, Letters of the New Testament, and documents of the post Apostolic age effectively turned their back on the image of Jesus given in the three Synoptic Gospels. The slain Lamb of God, raised as Lord over death and King of Creation, superceded the village prophet, humble teacher and compassionate healer. It is not that the church explicitly denied a mystery of lowliness in Jesus; rather, the church moved decisively to acclaim the Crucified, Risen and Ascended Lord as central to its faith and life and assigned only slight importance to the man of Nazareth. The question arises then as to what caused the change in emphasis.

The answer may never be certain. The process of substituting exaltation for lowliness was undoubtedly complex and there are few extant documents which help us understand the evolution of the early church's teaching and liturgical practice. Nevertheless, three factors can be indicated which almost certainly contributed to the change. The first came from Mediterranean culture; a second was the teachings of Paul the Apostle; and a third came with the evolution of the church.

Gerd Theissen, in his book "Social Reality and the Early Christians", provides helpful information on the first factor:

> Early Christianity initially came into being as an inner-Jewish revival movement in the rural areas of Palestine. But it spread pre-eminently as an independent religion, in the towns and cities of the Mediterranean world - that is, in places where the social conditions that had molded the Palestinian Jesus movement no longer existed. Yet it found an echo there. In the course of time, even the Synoptic traditions spread here too, although these traditions had their home in the Palestinian area.
>
> (235)

A few years after Jesus' death, the early Jesus Movement began to expand "pre-eminently as an independent movement" beyond Roman Palestine into the urban and gentile Mediterranean world. This was a context much different from the Jewish agricultural village communities of Galilee where the Movement originated. Theissen writes that there was a notable contrast in cultural milieu between that of the early followers of Jesus in Jewish Palestine and that of the new gentile converts in Graeco-Roman towns and cities. The first setting was predominantly rural and explicitly Hebrew in culture and religion; the second was urban and saturated with a multitude of Near Eastern religious persuasions and interests. The first setting fostered early Christian communities where many of the parables and sayings of Jesus were remembered, retold and eventually written down. The second setting produced communities in which the teachings of Paul the Apostle dominated, and in which the Fourth Gospel and some epistles of the New Testament later emerged.

In the Mediterranean world, excluding Jewish Palestine, the early Jesus movement faced a challenging religious environment. The various divinities - Egyptian, Persian, Greek and Roman - were believed to have had miraculous births, to work great miracles, and to be able to bring humans at death to a final salvation from earthly tribulation. We may fairly assume that, in responding to this milieu, the church found it necessary to make claims for Jesus which would establish his authority as superior to that of other divinities. It was a religiously competitive environment. The doctrine of a Risen and Ascended Lord could match rival claims made for the gods and goddesses of the various religious cults, some of whose power was also ascribed to an annual descent to Hades, death and supernatural resurrection. Similarly, Christian claims for Jesus' virgin birth echoed and compared well with widespread belief in the virgin births of such notables as Alexander and Augustus, not to mention similar claims for saviour figures in various religious cults. (Greater detail concerning classical Mediterranean religions and their importance for the newly emerging Jesus Movement is given in Appendix A.)

In this context of religious saturation, Christians would have found it difficult to persuade the general public that a humble and troublesome Jewish prophet of Galilee, who had been crucified as a common criminal, was indeed the Saviour of the world. Jesus of Nazareth as a mystery of lowliness would have had little persuasive evangelical force in this rude and dangerous world where arrogant and strident power held sway. The early church's interests would certainly have suffered puzzled resistance to the language of lowliness about their Lord, even among Christians themselves. In fact, we have clear evidence that the Apostle Paul himself had problems in persuading new Christian converts to believe in a humble Savior.

Writing to the congregation in Corinth, Paul sought to counter a negative response in the congregation to Jesus' humiliation in a criminal's death. He makes a bold and paradoxical claim in 1 Cor 1:18-25:

> For the message about the cross is foolishness to those who are perishing, but to us who are being saved it is the power of God. . . Has not God made foolish the wisdom of the world? For since, in the wisdom of God, the world did not know God through wisdom, God decided through the foolishness of our proclamation to save those who believe. For Jews demand signs and Greeks desire wisdom, but we proclaim Christ crucified, a stumbling block to Jews and foolishness to Gentiles, but to those who are the called, both Jews and Greeks, Christ the power of God and the wisdom of God. For God's foolishness is wiser than human wisdom, and God's weakness is stronger than human strength.

Within the Corinthian church there were factions competing against one another: "It has been reported to me by Chloe's people that there are quarrels among you". There was a power struggle in the congregation among adherents to different groups claiming to be loyal to Paul, Apollos, Cephas or Christ. There was little if any recognition that lowliness and mutual service were inherent in Christian faith and life. Members of the Corinthian church resisted believing in, or perhaps had not heard of, the "foolishness" and the "weakness" of the God who is revealed in the crucified Jesus. Paul found it necessary to underline this clear implication of the disgrace present in the way Jesus died and to claim it as a credit rather than a deficit for the new Christian faith. But there is little evidence in the Corinthian church correspondence that he succeeded in this endeavour.

Fascinating evidence of an apparent need to present a powerful Christianity to the unconverted comes from Pomerania in the 8th century. A missionary named Bernard had no success in converting this nation and as a consequence he advised the German Bishop Otto of Bamburg as follows:

> That foolish people, ignorant of the truth, saw my poverty and the wretchedness of my clothes and thought that I had come there not through love of Christ but because of my own needs. So they disdained to hear the word of salvation from me and sent me away. If you, dear father, wish to make any gains in the brute hearts of these barbarians, you must go there with a noble retinue of companions and servants and a plentiful supply of food and clothing. Those who, with unbridled neck, despised the yoke of humility will bow their necks in reverence for the glory of riches.
>
> (R. Fletcher, "The Barbarian Conversion",458)

This was written long after the time of the early church. But is it not very likely that those early Christians also experienced something similar to what Bernard found, that they too came to feel the need for a MIGHTY LORD, one who could out power the rival divinities of the day, claim the loyalty of many hearts, and reign as supreme? In fact, during the second and third centuries the Risen and Victorious Lord Jesus Christ became entrenched in mainstream Christian teaching, liturgy and devotion. An important exception to this trend was present in the early martyrs, but their witness - even though venerated - was not a major influence in the formation of doctrine about the Christ. In the pedagogy of Christian formation, the village man of Nazareth was scarcely evident. Within the violent culture of the Roman Empire, preaching the Ascended Lord and eternal King in heaven took precedence over testimony to the harried and humble prophet of Galilee.

A second factor, which contributed to the gradual ascendency of the Christological language of exaltation over the language of lowliness, is found in the teaching of the Apostle Paul. I have already quoted the famous passage from 1 Corinthians 1 where he pointed to the suffering and the exaltation of Jesus as two dimensions of one life. He sought the same balance in another well-known passage in his letter to Christians at Philippi, where he probably was quoting an early Christian hymn:

> Christ Jesus, who, though he was in the form of God, did not regard equality with God as something to be exploited, but emptied himself, taking the form of a slave . . . and became obedient to the point of death – even death on a cross. Therefore God has highly exalted him and gave him the name which is above every name, so that at the name of Jesus every knee should bend, in heaven and on earth and under the earth . . .
>
> (Phil 2:6-10)

Paul's customary language about Jesus is dramatic. "Christ redeemed us from the law by becoming a curse for us" (Gal.3:13); "if we have died with Christ, we believe that we will also live with him" (Rom.6:7); "Christ crucified, a stumbling block to Jews and foolishness to Gentiles . . . Christ the power of God and the wisdom of God" (1 Cor 1:23-24). Both humiliation and exaltation find a place in Paul's language. But his letters dwell more than anything else upon the benefits and blessings for Christians of the crucifixion/resurrection and have nothing to say about the historical Jesus' words and deeds.

Paul never knew the man of Nazareth. Paul's entry into Christian faith was "through a revelation of Jesus Christ" two or three years after Jesus' death.

> For I want you to know, brothers and sisters, that the gospel that was proclaimed by me is not of human origin: for I did not receive it from a human source, nor was I

86

taught it, but I received it through a revelation of Jesus Christ."

(Gal. 1: 11-12)

Nowhere does Paul refer to Jesus' public ministry, to his teaching and healing work, to his emphasis on the coming Reign of God. Paul calls the Gentiles to believe in a Risen, Ascended and Glorified Lord whose imminent return in glory was to be anticipated by the church. Faith and new life in this Lord Jesus is the constant burden of Paul's teaching. The lowliness of Jesus is certainly present in Paul's message, but it is there merely as the background against which he accents the victory of the crucified and risen Lord.

Subsequent generations of Christian teachers have found ample support in Paul for their own need to exalt Christ Jesus as Saviour and Redeemer. Orthodox Christianity made a decisive shift away from the picture presented in the Synoptic Gospels. Gospel stories about the teacher, healer and preacher from Nazareth were regarded as only preliminary to, and superseded in significance by, his death on a cross and its triumphant fulfilment in resurrection and ascension to heaven. Paul's writings have been a constant inspiration to this ongoing development, as is clearly documented in the writings of the early church Fathers and in theologians of every age.

A third factor moving early Christianity towards the exaltation of Jesus as Lord and Saviour came as a result of the evolution of the early Jesus Movement into a formal church structure. In Mark's gospel we read about Jesus' disciples James and John asking of him, "Grant us to sit, one at your right hand and one at your left, in your glory." Jesus indicated this was not possible, and later he said to the Twelve:

> You know that among the Gentiles those whom they recognize as their rulers lord it over them, and their great ones are tyrants over them. But it is not so among you; but whoever wishes to become great among you must be your servant, and whoever wishes to be first among you must be slave of all.

(Mark 10:42-44)

It is arguable that of all Jesus' teachings, this is the one in which the church has failed most consistently. This teaching contradicts the ways of the world; it requires a radical rejection of customary ways of exercising leadership in human society. During the time when the early church was shaping its teachings about Jesus there appears to have been an irresistible pressure to minimize this precept of the Master and to conform the patterns of authority in the church to those in the world.

History confirms that there was widespread neglect in the church of Jesus' teaching about servant leadership. Hierarchical, patriarchal and authoritarian leadership gradually became the norm even though there have always been notable exceptions - like the martyr Polycarp, first Bishop of Smyrna; Basil of Caesarea, a self-effacing monk and bishop of the fourth century; Bishop Francis de Sales in the 16th century; and, in our own time, Archbishop Oscar Romero of El Salvador. But as the institutional power structures gained prominence in the church, so awareness of the lowliness of Jesus faded from the minds of most of the faithful. The church's predominant memory of him became fixed in the sacred myth of the exalted and eternal Lord Jesus Christ. This Saviour of the world was declared to reign in power over his church and to delegate his own authority to the emerging clerical caste - those who are ordained into Holy Orders. It has been natural and all too human for leaders of the church to find it more convenient, to say the least, to perceive themselves as receiving their authority from a Risen and Triumphant Christ rather than from a servant prophet who ended up crucified.

The choice of early Christians to present an exalted Lord in the teaching, devotions and liturgies of the church has had immeasurable consequences for both church and world history. Most notably, the church has been able to sanctify power in its religious and social uses. Believing that eternal power had been given by God to the Christ, and from him to his church, ecclesiastical authorities have seen their own power as God-given. They have frequently claimed and tried to enforce intellectual, spiritual and political entitlement within various cultures right up to the present. Ironically, the cross, a clear emblem of weakness and disgrace, has been lifted up as the sign of ecclesial power, a declaration of sovereign authority to be exercised by Christians over other people. For centuries Western people have believed that the church and the

88

society it baptizes and sanctifies are authorized by the Christ to go and do all things in his holy name. And they did!

The (ab)use of power often turned out to be savagely inhuman and wantonly destructive. Some examples: the crusades of the 11th and 12th centuries, various expressions of the Inquisition during the 13th to 16th centuries, ruthless conquest of the Americas beginning in the 16th century, 19th century European imperialism in every part of the globe, the early 20th century American missionary slogan, "the world for Christ in our generation" (read: religion Western style), arrogant attempts to eliminate aboriginal religions, centuries of anti-semitism, a ubiquitous practice of male power and female submission - all this and more has been done in the name of the "King of kings and Lord of lords".

A clear statement about this tragic aspect of church history and Christian teaching was made in 1989 by Third World Christian theologians. Concerning their document, "The Road to Damascus", they say: "Hundreds of Christians have been involved in the preparation of this document, and thousands of us have chosen to sign it." In this document they write with dismay, sorrow, and anger:

> The God whom the missionaries preached to us was a God who . . . . dwelt in heaven and in the Temple but not in the world.
>
> The Jesus who was preached to us was barely human. He seemed to float above history, above all human problems and conflicts. He was pictured as a high and mighty king or emperor who ruled over us, even during his earthly life, from the heights of his majestic throne. His approach to the poor was therefore thought of as condescending. He condescended to make the poor the objects of his mercy and compassion without sharing their oppression and their struggles. His death had nothing to do with historical conflicts, but was a human sacrifice to placate an angry God. What was preached to us was a completely other-worldly Jesus who had no relevance to this life.
>
> These were the images of God and Jesus that we inherited from our conquerors and the missionaries who accompanied them.
>
> (sections 30 to 32)

The time is long since due for the Christian church to abandon this unhappy distortion which still afflicts our common life.

The chief doctrinal root of the language of exaltation and all it has implied for the false claims and lamentable actions of the church is to be found in the teaching of Jesus as the Lamb of God. If there is to be a departure in Christianity from the language of exaltation and all its tragic works, and a renewed appreciation of Jesus as a mystery of lowliness, there will have to be a clear recognition that there is no need for an act of atoning reconciliation between the human and the Divine.

And this takes us directly to another and deeper shift which is needed in the content of Christian teaching. Behind the proclamation of Jesus as the propitiatory suffering servant and human/Divine Mediator lies the image of a God who is punitive in response to human sin. For a very long time a deep moral chasm was believed to exist between the human and the Divine, and to bridge that chasm a Saviour was found in Jesus the Christ. In recent decades, however, the image of a powerful and punitive God has become obsolete for a great many Western people, and with that demise we have lost the need for a doctrine of the reconciling Lamb of God. Alternative images of God have been available for centuries, images which hark back to the compassionate Holy One of the Hebrew prophets.

A CHURCH LESS VISIBLE

The Doctrine of the Atonement is written large in history because it has been taught everywhere the church has gone. It stands out clearly in the Christian story and in Western culture. Many people have been persuaded that here we have the centre not only of the Christian story but also of the human story. Today, however, it is a troubled legacy whose time is past.

Less often mentioned in discussions about the church, but ultimately more significant for the well-being of society, are the lives of ordinary people in whom the rich spiritual resources of the Hebrew-Christian tradition have made their mark. In Negro spirituals and folk hymns, in famous paintings of domesticity and people at work, in books like "A Pilgrim's Progress" and "The Imitation of Christ", in stories like those by George Herbert, Elizabeth Goudge and Madeleine L'Engle - in a multitude of ways we learn that, through the centuries, Christian faith

90

entered into the daily round to nurture beauty, truth and goodness.

In social history the importance of Christian conscience can be seen. Catherine of Siena, George Fox, Charles Kingsley, Elizabeth Fry, Philip Berrigan, Dorothy Day, Desmond Tutu - a very long list could be made of Christians who have challenged the deficiencies and inequities of society, and urged the values of Christian social order.

In the congregational life of the church we find signs of faithful discipleship. A clergy friend once said to me, "In this fractious parish there are four older women whose presence keeps us from falling apart." This statement was a thoughtful appreciation of a quiet faithfulness in which compassion constantly reached out to heal pain, distress and confusion.

In all these kinds of Christian living the prophetic impulse becomes visible; here truth and compassion work the deep soil of the church's spiritual life, a sign of Sacred Presence.

In past centuries a literal reading of the Bible was common in Christianity. But today, more than at any previous time, we know that this book requires very careful interpretation. Many former interpretations are now seen to be inadequate; but this fact does not cancel out the positive contribution which the Bible made to the spiritual life of uncounted numbers of people. For nearly two thousand years, the stories of the Bible have gifted each generation with a feeling for the Sacred. The Christ Myth, like all great myths of humanity, has had its down side, its perversions and negative consequences. But it also sustained a rich culture and contributed spiritual depth to human life.

Much of this creativity has been due to the prophetic impulse in the church, to a continuing and quiet nurture of vital Christian discipleship. By its very nature this impulse is not noisy but is grounded in a mystery of lowliness. We can rejoice, then, that it is evident again in our own time, making itself felt in diverse ways. One of its most significant expressions is in contemporary biblical scholarship which is developing a picture of Jesus of Nazareth unsullied by the difficult associations of classical atonement Christology. Today, in Jesus, we are discovering that the ancient Hebrew social vision was reaffirmed and extended, that faith in the compassionate God was demonstrated. We are also rediscovering the sublime mystical tradition of the church which developed through many centuries in response to the person of the risen Jesus.

Though the formal faith tradition of Christendom is in decline, these less visible legacies of the church are already making a substantial contribution to the emerging new Story.

CHAPTER SUMMARY

In the early decades of the Jesus Movement, before clear lines of an institutional church had appeared, there were two differing traditions about Jesus which found a place in Christian practice. In Roman Palestine, stories about the humble servant prophet of Nazareth inspired small, local groups of disciples of the Way. But in Syria, Asia and Greece, under the influence of the Apostle Paul, teaching about the saving work of the crucified and risen Lord seem to have been central. How and when these two traditions met and fused is not known, but evidence of their respective development and partial integration is present in the New Testament.

From the later documents of the New Testament and other writings of the second century it is clear that the image of the crucified and risen Saviour of the world became dominant. A language of exaltation developed which obscured Jesus as a 'mystery of lowliness'. As Christian leaders took up the task of defining the church's faith, the eternal Christ who is seated at the right hand of the Father emerged as central in teaching, liturgy and devotion. Power in heaven and power in earth became ascribed to the Christ and to his church. This power was formally established and became widely extended after the church was officially recognized and accepted by the Emperor Constantine. And as Western society extended its influence into every corner of the world, the church exercised increasing influence not only in religious affairs but also in social and economic life.

The post-Constantinian church understood itself to be empowered by God not only for propagating its gospel message but also for leadership in the affairs of the world. The temptations of power proved to be strong and corrupting, and the example of Jesus as the humble servant prophet was almost lost from sight. Throughout the centuries, an expanding religious institution accumulated to itself wealth and temporal powers which often hindered communicating its own message and had destructive consequences for society at large. The Protestant Reformation originated in part as a critique of the medieval church's abuse of power, but in the long term itself fell into comparable patterns of institutional life.

These unfortunate characteristics of the church found their doctrinal roots in the image of Jesus as Saviour of the world, Lamb of God, King of Creation. This is the dominant tradition in Christianity. But another image of Jesus - servant prophet, healer and teacher - has lived on quietly among Christians in many places, inspiring a continuous flow of communities large and small who exemplified in their lives this truthful image of the Master. This is the prophetic impulse in the church. Throughout the ages many Christian people have been nurtured and sustained by this current of faithfulness, and today there are signs that this impulse is gaining strength, to give quiet leadership to a renewal of faith and practice.

A SENSE OF THE SACRED

Christopher Smart was irrepressible, he was unguarded, he was willing to play the holy fool, to proclaim that God was in his cat and therefore in everything else, too. He was writing from the far side of daily life where the world appears mysterious and unfamiliar, where everything trembles with divine presence, where every routine seems marvelous and every action is imbued with the sacred.

Edward Hirsch, "How To Read a Poem"

SCIENCE AND THE NEW COSMOLOGY

One of the most significant scientific discoveries in the last 125 years is the mutuality and interchange between energy and mass throughout the universe. We are accustomed to think of matter as solid. But science now teaches us that matter in its basic molecular structure is an extremely high-speed process in which energy and mass are constantly interchanging. At the micro level of the universe, mass is being created and destroyed in an endless exchange of energy. Energy is also a central determining factor in the macro cosmos, in the formation and behaviour of galaxies, stars and planets. Science now documents four fundamental kinds of energy which appear to determine how the universe continues in existence. Two of these relate to the macro cosmos of the expanding universe and two to the micro cosmos of molecular structure.

An equally significant development in scientific theory is the realization that the universe has been constantly evolving over some fifteen billion years. Everything in the expanding universe, from the smallest to the largest, was already present within the originating flaring forth. Everything was implicit in that beginning, each phenomenon waiting for its turn to appear throughout eons of time. Philosophers of science speak of the exquisitely beautiful and dramatically eloquent manner in which the universe has evolved itself through successive stages, each of which is still being documented in detail by scientific investigation. "The story of the universe is a story of majesty and beauty as well as of violence and disruption, a drama filled with both elegance and ruin" (Swimme and Berry, "The Universe Story", 47). There has been a wondrous unfolding of succeeding patterns of energy/mass, from elementary gases to the formation of billions of galaxies, and then trillions upon trillions of stars, among which is our sun with its planets, including Earth.

The evolution of Earth from its beginning to the present has taken about four billion years. The first segment of this time was taken for the cooling of flaming gases and molten rock, a gradual calming of a seething cauldron of activity to form land masses and seas. Chemicals present in the seas produced organic material from which emerged myriad life forms of increasing complexity. About 114 million years ago the first placental mammals appeared, with the species *homo* appearing about two and one half million years ago.

We have heard much about the struggle for survival in the evolution of Earth, a so-called 'survival of the fittest'. This, however, is not the only way to speak about the emergence of each species from its predecessors. The process can also be described as a delicately designed collaboration in which species becoming extinct yield their existence to provide the material base for those which follow. Though nature appears to be 'red in tooth and claw', a more profound reading of the process may reveal a constant series of creative sacrifice so that later forms appear from the earlier or, in more mundane terms, may provide the material foundation for the later. The biologist William Trager commented, "the 'fittest' may be the one that helps another to survive."

In this model of the cosmos, evolution is understood to be a process of continuing diversification, of increasing complexity and differentiation. The process moves constantly from simpler to more complex forms. For example: the cosmos, at least within Earth's systems, shows itself to be constantly achieving ever higher forms of psychic activity. Elementary neural matter evolves into nervous systems which require specialized cranial structures. These in turn promote more complex cranial matter. Eventually the brain of mammalian life appears, bringing to Earth a high form of consciousness. There seems to be an insistent thrust in this process which propels cosmic reality toward increasingly explicit consciousness, and ultimately to the self-consciousness of *homo sapiens*. Some philosophers of nature suggest that 'inwardness' was implicit from the beginning: Teilhard de Chardin named this 'the within'.

The danger in describing evolution in this way is an implication that the cosmic process intended to reach fulfilment in the human species. A more objective claim states that through rational creatures, on Earth and perhaps elsewhere, the cosmos becomes able to reflect upon itself and thus to create the potential for intelligent choices to be made about its own future. In this way humans are seen to be part of one Story which has been unfolding for eons of time and will continue into the future, with or without us. This is a radically new cosmology within which to ponder human existence and its meaning.

OUR THEOLOGICAL LEGACY AND CLASSICAL COSMOLOGY

Philosophers of nature who are not engaged by religious questions find the new cosmology a self-sufficient account of the universe as we experience it today. For them, to raise the question of God is both unnecessary and intrusive. But for other seekers after truth, cosmic reality points to an intrinsic mystery of the Sacred and they ask how the new cosmology relates to traditional religious faith. In pursuing this question in the context of European culture, however, a major obstacle appears because traditional Hebrew-Christian discourse is deeply marked by a cosmology which is now obsolete. The symbolism of our religious culture has become alien to the symbolism being generated by science.

The Hebrew-Christian religious tradition emerged within the culture of the ancient Near East. The cosmology of that culture visualized a flat Earth with a concave heavenly firmament above and a dark underworld beneath. The heavenly bodies, sun and moon and planets, were set in a series of spherical layers between Earth and the heavenly firmament which was the realm of the Divine. It was a closed system. The gods lived in heaven; between the gods and Earth were many levels of supernatural powers with varying abilities to influence human affairs. The God of the ancient Hebrew people, Yahweh, through the triumph of Hebrew-Christian religion in the Roman Empire, eventually came to be seen as superior to all other divinities and to reign on high as Lord and eternal King, Judge and Saviour of the world.

All the biblical images of the Hebrew deity and of the way He (firmly patriarchal) works are premised on this cosmology. In time these images became central also to the Christian religion. God is 'up there', and He dispenses divine wrath against human sin and bestows divine beneficence at least in part in response to human petitions and acts of devotion. God is eternal, absolute, sovereign and arbitrary; humanity is temporal, contingent and dependent. And the distance between God and humanity is not only one of essence, of quality of being; it is also one of moral distance. God is holy and we are sinful. To overcome this separation, the Christian church elaborated a doctrine of salvation through the divinely-appointed self-sacrifice of Jesus the Christ on a cross, who now lives as God with God on high.

Everything in the religious imagery of classical Christian teaching, liturgy and devotions is coloured by classical cosmology. Consequently, some modern people, who know themselves to be part of a very different cosmic Story, find in the classical imagery of the Hebrew-Christian tradition a disconcerting lack of meaning. Traditional symbolism no longer works for them.

Though classical Christian faith is frequently expressed in archaisms which have lost their meaning for some contemporary people, we can and should distinguish between the external forms and the spiritual content which those forms intended to convey. We must distinguish between the heart and the husk. Consider prayer for example. The language, music, dance and drama of prayer (the forms in which prayer is expressed) are deeply conditioned by images of the Divine present in the believing community in each time and place. Traditional forms of prayer still in use today continue to be determined by cultural forces now lost to us. So, for at least some of us, the inner forces which drive us to pray no longer find adequate expression in the external forms which are provided by our tradition. We are pressed to invent new vehicles for the expression of our spiritual energies. When we pray, we find it necessary to change our symbolism of the Sacred.

The heart of spiritual wisdom lies deep in humanity's encounter with

97

our physical environment. The spiritual fruits of that encounter constantly seek appropriate forms in which to articulate themselves. And when an existing mode of symbolism fails to be adequate in power and eloquence for that task, humans struggle to find new symbolism which can express their sense of the Sacred.

What is unsaid above is that each generation is tutored in spiritual life by its predecessor. Tutors expect that pupils will find the received forms for expressing spiritual experience just as eloquent for themselves as it continues to be for the tutors. But periodically there is discontinuity - bringing dismay to the tutors and challenge to the pupils. And unfortunately, even mutual respect between tutors and pupils does not necessarily lessen the inevitable confusion, nor the potential for misunderstanding and hurt.

Our forebears in faith had little choice in the symbolism they used to express their experience of the Sacred; they were restricted to the rich cultural images which were at hand. How, then, shall we receive the spiritual wisdom which for centuries was conveyed more or less effectively in the old symbol system? To the extent that this is possible and desirable, we can accomplish this transition only by finding symbolism suitable for our own time in which to express the wisdom of the past as part of our own spiritual experience. There is, of course, no guarantee of coherence between past and present - there is always a risk that something will be lost. Nevertheless, we must find effective ways to express what we are experiencing or it will lie mute within us. Since the old symbolism is no longer adequate we must invent the new.

As we today attempt to mythologize our own inner Truth - Truth which is always evolving and can never stand naked before us - we turn naturally to the cultural options of our own time. One source of help for this task comes from the new Story of the universe, the new cosmology, from its vital images and symbols. Here we shall find new religious language, liturgy, arts and actions to guide our response to Sacred Presence and bring new fulfilment to ourselves as part of planet Earth.

CONTEMPORARY THEOLOGY AND THE NEW COSMOLOGY

Ecological theologian Thomas Berry and physicist Brian Swimme have given us a book titled "The Universe Story". They discuss the unfolding Story of the universe, beginning with the initial flaring forth and continuing through the evolution of planet Earth to its multiple life forms. They tell how the cosmos has transformed itself step by step in a manner both amazing and marvellous, a process which appears to involve "self-direction".

> The universe established its fundamental physical interactions in a manner similar to the way it unfurled its space – with stunning elegance. Had it settled on a slightly different strong interaction [i.e. stronger than existing gravity], all future stars would have exploded in a brief time, making an unfurling of life impossible. Had the universe established a slightly different [lesser] gravitational interaction, none of the future galaxies would have taken shape. The integral nature of the universe is revealed in its actions. The universe as it expands itself and establishes its basic coherence reveals the elegance of activity necessary to hold all the immensely complex possibilities of its future blossoming .
>
> (19)

The authors repeatedly indicate the narrow tolerances within which each major step of evolutionary development proceeded and outside of which the expansion of the universe would have been aborted. "The universe maintained itself on a knife edge"(24). "Only a coordinated sequence of transitions makes possible the emergence of entirely new realities"(70). ".... micro-organisms took what was waste for one kind of being and discovered that it could become food for another kind of being .... the wild wisdom at the heart of the universe story"(89). And when discussing the evolution of life, these authors wonder about the place of "choice" in contrast to the self-propelling process of natural selection:

> Perhaps natural selection and genetic mutation are primary within a relatively fixed environment with relatively stable species. . . . Perhaps it is only in the major evolutionary changes, such as the invasion of land, that conscious choice becomes the primary cause explaining the change"
>
> (132).

By means of these and many other examples, the authors suggest that we should "accept the process [of the unfurling of the universe] as a sacred context for existence and meaning" (251-2). "Presently we are moving beyond any religious expression so far known to the human into a meta-religious age that seems to be a new comprehensive context for all religions" (255). They are proposing the need for *a new myth* which can inherit the wisdom of past cosmic myths, extending and correcting them in the light of modern scientific understanding.

Are we now in the historical moment when insights coming from scientific paradigms of cosmic evolution, and insights found in the spiritual wisdom of the great religious traditions, can enter into fruitful dialogue and exchange? Can the energies of the evolving cosmos be said to have an internal spiritual dimension which holds meaning and purpose, both for the cosmos as a whole and for human life in particular? David Toolan ("At Home in the Cosmos",175) reports that some physicists believe that "from the first nanosecond [of the Big Bang] - against all probability - the cosmos has been so arranged as to make the emergence of life a high probability." And when self-consciousness developed within human life we arrived at the cusp of the spiritual.

The cosmic energies, in their self-expression as sentient being, we name 'life'. When this life developed into human life it acquired the unique characteristic of reflective self-consciousness. It is our reflective self-consciousness which allows and invites humans to ponder the meaning of the cosmos. It is reflective self-consciousness which gives us the experience of self-transcendence: we can imagine worlds beyond the one we daily enjoy. And in that pondering and in that imagining there has emerged, as though from deeply within the cosmic process itself, human awareness and affirmation of the Sacred.

From time immemorial there have been humans with a highly developed awareness of the cosmic Sacred. These have been the shamans, the prophets, the seers, the wise women and men of diverse cultures. They affirm experiences of 'being addressed' by the Sacred in Earth and its creatures, and from within their own personal being - from a 'centre' which is sometimes designated 'soul'. They affirm a spiritual journey taken in response to Sacred Presence. And their lives and their teachings have become stepping stones for others who are seeking to respond to their own sense of Sacred Presence. For Christians, Jesus of Nazareth is pre-eminent in that large company.

The experience in the human of 'being addressed' by the Sacred gives rise to a sense of the Sacred within cosmic energies as possessing a 'personal' dimension - though not being a person. And from the experience of 'being addressed' each human may discover herself or himself as a unique expression of those same energies, as a material/spiritual 'subject' with personal reality. Thus, each man and each woman is capable of a profound relationship with the Sacred. The traditional name for this possibility is 'communion' with the Divine, with the Holy One.

This line of reasoning can be expressed in another way. Humans have named the sacred Presence who addresses us as Mystery, Word, Light - signifying works of intuition, hearing and seeing. But such terms are merely symbolic and can never define the hidden spiritual quality of the cosmic energies. God-in-essence is unknowable to human beings. The "within" (T. de Chardin) of the cosmic energies lies beyond our rational comprehension. Nevertheless, experience allows us to claim that this Presence, as self-expressed in the cosmos and within human consciousness, desires to be known by us. In principle, some form of union is possible between the particularity of the self-conscious human spirit and the universality of the cosmic energies as personal. In fact, union of the human spirit with the Divine is often felt to be actual. It is this experience which forms the heart of the mystical tradition.

The argument is inevitably circular. On the one hand, there are data which scientific investigation has gathered about the vast physical extent of the universe and about random patterns of energy/mass in ceaseless motion which form its foundational structure. On the other hand, there are data from human consciousness, identified and valued as intimations of Sacred Presence. When and how do these two sets of data meet and enrich each other? Neither set of data necessarily implies the other, but each may be seen to be consistent with the other. And when we link them together within what might be called our 'search for meaning', they seem to fit rather well.

RECOVERING A SENSE OF THE EARTH AS SACRED

Recurring experiences of the Sacred: these are at the heart of the biblical Story. For the ancient Hebrews, and much later and in a different way for the first Christians, stories about experiences of Sacred Presence became embedded in community memory. And as this extensive memory was ritually rehearsed in sacred liturgy it became the core of the biblical tradition.

Though the Divine remained always and entirely hidden, the Divine was continually making Itself known. Israel was frequently surprised by the leading of the Holy One. So also were the early followers of Jesus, who spoke frequently of the Indwelling Spirit guiding them. And it is instructive to note that in many of these stories, human/Divine encounter was associated with something in nature. A listing of important examples will illustrate this point:

- Moses senses the presence of his God as his attention is drawn to a bush which appears to be on fire but is not consumed

(Exodus 3:1ff).

- Balaam's ass 'speaks' to his master to call his attention to the presence of an angel of the Lord who is barring their way on the road

(Num 22:21ff).

- Elijah's contest with prophets of the Ba'al is won through a manifestation of the Divine in a violent storm

(1 Kgs:18:20 ff).

- Hosea marries a prostitute upon instructions from Yahweh as the means by which the prophet will enter upon a new understanding of God

(Hos 1:2)

- Amos, wandering in the market, sees some rotten summer fruit and becomes aware that Yahweh is showing him Israel's true moral state

(Amos 8:1ff).

- Jeremiah notices a potter shaping his clay and realizes the Yahweh 'shapes' the destiny of the people Israel

(Jer 18:2 ff).

- scribal editors, possibly during the 6th century BCE, add to Israel's evolving religious tradition their vision of Yahweh's act of creating Earth: "And God saw everything that he had made and it was very good"

(Gen 1:31).

- Jesus of Nazareth is baptized by John in the waters of

the River Jordan   (Mk 1:9)

- Peter is won to Jesus through a miraculous catch of fish
                                                    (Lk 5ff)

- Saul the Pharisee is temporarily blinded by a brilliant
light.   (Acts 9:3)

In each of these events the material order mediates an awareness of the Sacred; but mediating Sacred Presence is not the same as being intrinsically sacred. In the earliest times of the biblical Hebrews all of Nature was felt to be intrinsically sacred, an experience characteristic of all Near Eastern religions of that time. Israel, however, gradually moved away from this view and eventually her sense of the Sacred was chiefly found in Yahweh God's actions in history. This gradual alienation from Nature was reinforced in Christianity where the significance of Jesus was seen only in terms of human history moving towards its fulfilment in God.

For most Westerners it is a long journey back in mind and heart to rediscover a sacred Earth which has been discarded by our profane and profaning culture. We are children of a legacy with three impulses which have reduced our perception of Earth to a source of raw materials provided for human use. First, there is our religious tradition, where God is Lord of creation but has no obvious connection with the cyclical life of Nature apart from sustaining it - presumably from a remote eternity. Moreover, this God is believed to have created the human as the pinnacle of the divine work so that humankind may have dominion over it. As an early Christian theologian, Irenaeus, put it, "The glory of God is the human fully alive" - and everything else is made to serve the human. Second, there is the philosophical legacy of ancient Greece with its dualisms of matter and spirit, body and mind, temporal and eternal. Our cultural legacy trains us to make these separations, and one result has been that we view Earth as (lowly) raw material to be investigated and manipulated by (superior) human minds. And finally, there is our present enveloping technological economy which has been expanding into every corner of Earth to harness raw material to meet our insatiable desire for human comfort and well-being. It is difficult for us to recover a sense of reverence for Earth when for centuries we have been trained to approach it as an object for use.

It is difficult, but it is not impossible. And today, in a new cosmology, we have a tutor for our mental and spiritual transformation. As Thomas Berry observes, we can discover that "we live inside a Story", the sacred Story of an unfolding cosmic drama of which we are an integral part. He suggests that the universe itself is a kind of liturgy - a dramatic enactment of sacred Story. We need, therefore, to re-imagine and re-invent the human as integral to a cosmic reality in which every part is connected with every other part in life-giving relationships. We can learn to appreciate Earth as "a communion of subjects, not a collection of objects".

That is how Thomas Berry believes we must see Earth. When human beings regard Earth as a collection of objects, we consider ourselves to be the priniciple subjects with rights over the objectified Earth and its many creatures. On the other hand, when we regard Earth as a communion of subjects, everything participates in the Sacred and all parts are seen to be inter-connected.

Some years ago I was at a conference held in an Aboriginal Centre. As part of the program we were invited to share in a traditional 'sweat', held in the sweat lodge on site. Eight of us took our places within the low circular lodge and, after sharing in each of the four cycles of song and prayer offered by the leader, we were offered the opportunity to pray, always concluding with the words, "And all my relations". As I learned some time later, one of the central teachings in Aboriginal culture is the inter-connectedness of all things. Each human is related to every other living thing and to all material forms that comprise Earth; and everything, absolutely everything, carries the imprint of the Sacred. All these are "my relations".

A sense of the Sacred in everything was integral to human consciousness for most of human history. Anthropologists sometimes refer to this long period as the time of a primitive naiveté, a time when human capacity for abstract and analytical reasoning was still undeveloped and the human mind was immersed in a world full of immediacy and mystery. However, this naiveté - which is evident in mythologies of past ages - is now firmly behind us. Humanity has lived through several thousand years in which we have been learning to apply

104

our reason to virtually everything. We value our rationality highly and through it have discovered an exciting and rewarding ability for creative criticism. We cannot abandon this; but we can refuse to allow our high regard for this faculty to hold us back from a new depth of consciousness which is also available to us. We can adopt what has been termed a "post-critical naiveté" - a term I met first in the work of Paul Ricoeur. This second naiveté can release our thought and imagination from a sterile rationalism which would blind us to the reality of mystery in the cosmos.

A post-critical naiveté retains a capacity for critical reasoning but recognizes the limitations of rationality. This second naiveté understands that there are ways of knowing, vital and creative ways of knowing, which are non-rational but not irrational. Mystical awareness is rooted in this capacity. Affectivity, a feeling for the inner reality of phenomena, uses this capacity. A grasp of the inter-relatedness of everything, a sense of the whole, is a gift of the second naiveté.

Aboriginal people have very important traditional teachings to share with the rest of us as we try to wake up to a new, fruitful and humble awareness of the Earth in all its majesty and beauty. For us, the second naiveté can open us to a profound sense of the Sacred in all things and a readiness to honour an amazing mystery in the material processes of the entire cosmos. Thomas Berry suggests that Earth is a prime revelation of the Holy One precisely because the Sacred is the Matrix of cosmic matter, because the Sacred is the hidden inner structure of all material existence. It seems to me that these mystical intuitions are essential if humanity is to integrate itself successfully with the continuing evolution of Earth.

MYSTICISM AND THE SACRED

> But now you put a question to me asking, "How shall I think about God Himself, and what is He?" . . . He may be well loved, but he may not be thought of. He may be reached and held close by means of love, but by means of thought never. . . . you are to try to pierce that darkness which is above you. You are to strike that thick cloud of unknowing with a sharp dart of longing love; and you are not to retreat no matter what comes to pass.
>
> (13th century, anon
> "The Cloud of Unknowing", Chapter 6)

The Christian mystical tradition offers us some of the most profound human intuitions and experiences of Sacred Presence. Moreover, mysticism is to be found in every religious tradition; so that here we touch a stream of human experience which is universal. I cannot,however, in a short space, do any more than hint at what is meant by mysticism, in the hope that interested readers will be encouraged to look elsewhere for a more complete discussion.

A few selections from Evelyn Underhill's comprehensive volume, "Mysticism", give us a feeling for this work of the human spirit.

> "Mysticism is seen to be a highly specialized form of that search for reality, for heightened and completed life, which we have found to be a constant characteristic of human consciousness. It is largely prosecuted by that 'spiritual spark', that transcendental faculty which, though it is the life of our life, remains below the threshold in ordinary men *(sic)*. Emerging from its hiddenness in the mystic, that spiritual spark gradually becomes the dominant factor in his life; subduing to its service . . . those vital powers of love and will which we attribute to the head."
>
> (93)

> "The true mystic claims no promises and make no demands [of God]. He goes because he must, as Galahad went towards the Grail. . . . With Mechthild of Magdeburg, she hears the Absolute saying in her soul, 'O soul, before the world was I longed for thee: and I still long for thee, and thou for Me. Therefore, when our two desires unite, Love shall be fulfilled'."
>
> (92)

> "The mystics show us this independent spiritual life, this fruition of the Absolute, enjoyed with a fulness to which others cannot attain. They are the heroic examples of the life of spirit; as the great artists, the great discoverers, are the heroic examples of the life of beauty and the life of truth. Directly participating, like all artists, in the Divine life, they are usually persons of great vitality."
>
> (34)

> "as the object of the mystic's adventure . . . knowledge and communion are the same thing."
>
> (68)

"Erigena says, 'Every visible and invisible creature is a theophany or appearance of God' - as all might perhaps see it, if prejudice, selfhood, or other illusion did not distort our sight. From this loving vision there comes very often that beautiful sympathy with, that abnormal power over, all living natural things, which crops up again and again in the lives of the mystical saints. . . . It is surely not very amazing that St. Francis of Assisi, feeling and knowing - not merely 'believing' - that every living creature was veritably and actually a 'theophany or appearance of God', should have been acutely conscious that he shared with these brothers and sisters of his the great and lovely life of the All. . . . The true mystic, so often taunted with a 'denial of the world', does but deny the narrow and artificial world of self: and finds in exchange the secrets of that mighty universe which he shares with Nature and with God. Strange contacts, unknown to those who only lead the life of sense, are set up between his being and the being of all other things."

(260)

"'How', says the Disciple to the Master in one of Boehme's 'Dialogues', 'am I to seek in the Centre of this Fountain of Light which may enlighten me throughout and bring my properties into perfect harmony?' *Master*. Cease but from thine own activity, steadfastly fixing thine Eye upon *one Point* . . . . For this end, gather in all thy thoughts, and by faith press into the Centre."

(313)

Mysticism is more a process and method - a Way - than it is a particular body of teaching. The classical mystics cannot easily be gathered into schools of thought. And yet in common we find a spiritual discipline and single-minded search for union with Sacred Presence which places them apart from the ordinary pilgrim of the Way of Truth, Beauty and Goodness. On the other hand, the ordinary pilgrim is open to mystical awareness even though not endowed with the special graces that are evident in the authors of the great mystical treatises.

Evelyn Underhill wrote a book with an interesting title, "Practical Mysticism for Normal People." She offers a definition of mysticism:

Mysticism is the art of union with Reality. The mystic is a

person who has attained that union in greater or lesser degree; or who aims at and believes in such attainment.

(3)

Later she comments,

> the distinction between mystic and non-mystic is not merely that between the rationalist and the dreamer, between intellect and intuition. The question which divides them is really this: What, out of the mass of material offered to it, shall consciousness seize upon - with what aspects of the universe shall it 'unite'? (5) . . . . If the doors of perception were cleansed, said Blake, everything would appear to man*(sic)* as it is - Infinite. But the doors of perception are hung with the cobwebs of thought; prejudice, cowardice, sloth. Eternity is with us, inviting our contemplation perpetually.

(18)

Blake's 'Infinite' and 'Eternity' are equivalent in meaning to that which in contemporary language I signify by 'the Sacred'.

If, in our technologically-sophisticated age, we are truly to experience Nature as "a communion of subjects, not a collection of objects", then some trial of the mystical path seems an obvious choice to make, an adventure to be risked. Indeed, I suspect that the heart of the new Story will come as the fruits of our mystical knowing.

It is the vocation and genius of science - whether through the microscope, the stethoscope, the telescope, or other means - to discover, name and explain the dynamics of the universe. Science seeks to de-mystify as much of our world as possible and will insist that our search for a new Story be grounded in verifiable experience. But there are depths to our world which defy scientific explanation; there is an invisible wall encountered by science beyond which lies mystery. It is the vocation and genius of the arts and of religion to take us by mystical experience into those elements of reality which demand mythical - in contrast to analytical - expression. The new Story will only capture our hearts and wills as it successfully embodies the fruits of our mystical knowing and mythical telling.

BEING PRESENT TO THE SACRED

In humanity's ages-long spiritual journey, a great many ways have been found to be present to the Sacred. But now, at this juncture of our history, much of Western society's traditional devotional and liturgical language for this work has become unfamiliar and is being discarded. Many people, perhaps most, lack ways of articulating a sense of Sacred Presence, even when this overwhelms them. A significant challenge, then, is to explore new language and other symbolic expressions (dance, music, physical artifacts, natural objects, etc.) by which we open ourselves to Sacred Presence, prepare our hearts and minds for the incoming of the Divine, and celebrate all that we are receiving. In this work we are not in search of new dogmatic definitions, such as the classical religions have formulated over the last two or three thousand years. Our need is for new narratives, new poetry, new art forms which point to the sublime mystery of the Holy and break us open to its impact on our lives without our attempting to produce any final definitions.

Here are six explorations into language which seek to name Sacred Presence.

Sacred Mystery, creative Source of all that is.

To speak of 'Mystery' carries a strong suggestion that the Holy is beyond human comprehension. We are not addressing a commonplace presence; this is One before whom we are compelled to 'take off our shoes', to bend the knee.

To speak of the Sacred as 'creative Source' reflects the view of science that the cosmos came from a single initial flaring forth, the originating cosmic event. Everything which at this moment exists was present in potential at that creative beginning - everything, including ourselves. From that Source we are and from that Source we continue to be.

Divine Agapé, embracing every creature.

The Divine is indiscriminate in generosity: the divine goodwill embraces everything. This brings a two-fold challenge. The first is to accept this foundational truth for ourselves, to accept this unfathomable valuation of the human by the Divine into the centre of who we are. Each person is a singular work of grace called to receive, moment by moment, the constant flow of gifts which God bestows through the cosmic order. And what is true for us individually is more profoundly true when we are bound together in communities of love.

The second challenge is to reach out in deep respect to all other creatures as equal in value to ourselves and to respond to them accordingly.

Eternal Wisdom, speaking to our hearts.

One of the most profound mysteries of human experience is that of 'being addressed' by Sacred Presence. Biblical narratives give numerous examples of this which together express a single paradigm of human/Divine encounter, and each instance of this experience can only be understood when it is placed within its own historical context. Authentic hearing of the Word always leaves us changed in heart, mind and soul; it deepens our humility and strengthens our desire to respond in love to the needs of other creatures in the Earth community.

Passionate God, of uncounted blessings.

The Creator is urgently engaged with the Creation, moment by moment. This is not a remote, impersonal force; this is the Enlivening Breath of Love which never departs. Whenever we discover that we have departed from an awareness of the Holy One it is immediately possible to return and to be present. The dark side of our actions and of our experiences notwithstanding, the door to renewed healing and blessing is always open.

Wounded God, grieving for the brokenness of Earth and of her creatures.

There is a cost to the Holy One in loving the tortured Earth. Human categories fail completely to comprehend the mystery of the identification of Creator with creation in suffering love, but the cross of Jesus points to it. We are not alone in our sorrows; and we may, in some indescribable manner, be called to share in the divine grieving.

Immanent Spirit, moving in our history to overcome evil with Shalom.

The Holy One is not only the Beyond but is also the "Beyond in the midst" (Bonhoeffer), penetrating all. And this personal, saturating Presence is engaged with our history to bring righteousness and peaceable living in Earth, to give Shalom - the well-being of Earth and all its creatures. Concerning Shalom, the psalmist sings:

> "Mercy and faithfulness have met;
> justice and peace have embraced."

To accomplish Shalom, the Holy One enables humans to achieve our true being through the gift of indwelling divine love, best witnessed for Christians in the life, death and resurrection of Jesus of Nazareth.

To work with language such as this is to seek to be 'in the Presence'. We seek to place ourselves in relation to the Mystery of the Holy so that the human heart, mind and will may be brought into correspondence with the divine loving and purpose.

Simone Weil teaches us to come into the Presence "with attention and consent". By attention and consent the human ego becomes willing to accept its own diminishment so that the true self-in-God may live and grow. The goal of this kind of prayer is our transformation in mind, spirit and deed so that we may become persons able to assist in the transformation of the world, in accord with the divine purpose.

Words, images and concepts like those given above are instruments. They are designed to assist us - as we take time and make occasion - to be present and open to Sacred Presence. They will be most useful if we make trial use of them for ourselves, allowing ourselves to grow with them, to alter them, or to place them aside as not appropriate for our own spiritual journeys. And in all this work it is well to remember some counsel from Rabbi Abraham Heschel: "Prayer is not an accumulation of spiritual knowledge but a capacity to face the sacred moment."

If there is to be a new 'age of faith' ahead, it will come as we make time purposefully to seek to be open to Sacred Presence. In these times we have freedom to let the old die away and to allow the truly new to arrive.

Here the Holy One moves secretly to engage every part of our lives, and to reveal to us the Web of Sacred Life within which we are related to all other people and to the wider society of the other Earth creatures.

In our beginnings, You call us into a journey;
each day you invite us into new truth,
new goodness, new loving.

Holy One, You are present;
    throughout uncounted eons of the unfurling
    universe You have always been present.
The Mystery of your timeless Being
    meets the mystery of our searching hearts.
As we open ourselves to numinal Presence
    our restlessness is stilled,
    wounded lives find healing,
    sorrowing hearts find hope.
Hidden Heart of the Cosmos:
    we come to You with spiritual desire,
    with a deep interior hunger
    satisfied only by knowing and doing your will.
But how shall we find our way to your Shalom?
The planet writhes in agony;
    with perverse greed and insolence
    not known in any other creature
    humans despoil your handiwork.
To find our way,
    help us to accept the gift of your Presence.

CHAPTER SUMMARY

For several centuries the physical sciences have been making increasingly precise observations about the Cosmos and Earth. During recent decades this data has been interpreted to yield coherent stories which describe the physical context within which humanity has been formed and now lives. From the microcosm of nanology to the macrocosm of astrophysics, a new picture of the origins and structure of the universe is appearing.

In response to this work of the scientific community, philosophers and theologians are articulating a 'new cosmology'. Literally, cosmology means a 'wisdom about the cosmos', a wisdom which seeks to express the ultimate physical and spiritual origin and destiny of the human species.

This work has drastically altered the context in which the Christian church must understand and express its faith tradition. In its beginnings, Christianity assumed the Ptolemaic world view as given; this was the cosmology in which Earth was believed to be the centre of all physical reality. The church used metaphors and imagery drawn from that cosmology to develop its doctrines and create its liturgies. It is no surprise then that the classical teachings of the church largely fail to resonate with educated people today: much of the traditional symbolism no longer works.

Together with this basic liability, the church today has inherited a second liability - a view of the natural order as created for human benefit, as made for our manipulation and exploitation. While Aboriginal Peoples still retain a sense of Earth as sacred and as requiring respect, Western culture and Western religion view the Earth as available for human use and advantage. Within the context of a looming environmental crisis, Christianity is experiencing a wakeup call that demands the transformation of inherited convictions and teaching. "Earth is not a collection of objects; it is a communion of subjects." Thomas Berry's words can guide the development of a revolution in our relationships with Earth and all its creatures.

The mystical traditions of all world religions alert us to the human capacity for a deep spiritual union of human spirit with the sacred depths of Nature. The practice of mysticism need not be esoteric; every person is able in some degree to experience Sacred Presence. In this practice will lie the power of a new Story to gather all humanity into one global fabric of meanings.

CELEBRATING THE DIVINE GENEROSITY

Holy One, Holy and Gracious,
Eternal Wisdom, Nurturing Spirit,
You surround us, You indwell us,
You call our hearts to a communion of love
with Earth and all her creatures.
You draw us in love to yourself,
You teach our hearts to sing!

STORIES WITHIN STORIES

Throughout this book I have been using the word 'story' to apply variously to five different realities. These stories form a progression, like a series of envelopes where each one holds within itself all those which follow in the series, except for the last which is held within the others but contains only its own reality.

The Great Story of the cosmos, which began about fourteen billion years ago, is magnificent and astonishing beyond all imagination. The ever increasing diversification and complexity of the cosmos, and its constant extension through expanding space, is being revealed by science as a process with on going self-direction. It is the Great Story with its own plot, narrative and characters.

The Story of Earth is unfolding within the Great Story. In the galaxy known as the Milky Way, planet Earth was born about four billion years ago and has developed since then through a process with its own plot, narratives and characters. Scientists have given specific names to the geological periods of Earth, tracing how each developed from the one preceding. Each geological period made its own contribution to the evolution of Earth. The last 65 million years constitute the Cenozoic Period in which the more complex life forms have increasingly dominated the Story of Earth.

Within the Story of Earth we find our third story, the Story of Humanity. All tribes and nations, all ethnic groups and peoples, have a common origin story in the Stories of the Cosmos and of Earth. This origin story tells about the one common beginning of each and every strand of humanity in all its amazing diversity. And, as far as we can tell, it is within this third Story that a sense of Sacred Presence first makes its appearance.

In response to the natural world, the peoples of Earth learn how to support themselves from Earth's bounty and to create many kinds of communal living. Within this prodigious work of accomodation and invention there is in humanity a constant blending of active curiosity, transfixed wonderment, and awed fear in response to the natural environment. As human consciousness responds to and reflects upon its experience of the cosmos and of Earth, a sense of Sacred Presence emerges. Human beings become subjects of an awareness of "the numinous": experiences which yield "beliefs and feelings qualitatively different from anything that 'natural experience' is capable of giving us" (R. Otto,"The Idea of the Holy").

It is because of this universal feeling for the numinous, this aware-ness of Sacred Presence in response to Nature, that I give the word Earth a capital 'E'. I want to acknowledge that this beautiful planet mediates a sense of sacred mystery, that Earth declares Sacred Presence embedded in itself and in the entire cosmic process, a Presence seeking to make Itself known to us. This self-revelation of the Sacred within the temporal is the origin of religion.

The fourth in our succession of stories are the Stories of the great world religions as found in their sacred Scriptures and traditions. For Western society, the Hebrew Story is the most prominent among these.

Late in the Hebrew Story, the Jesus Movement emerged as a sect of first century Judaism. However, it remained within Judaism for only a short while before beginning its own independent story - the fifth in our series. In this book I have discussed only those parts of the Hebrew and Christian Stories which I believe are absolutely necessary for the present renewal of Christian faith and life.

This, then, is a pattern of five successive stories within stories: Cosmos, Earth, Humanity, ancient Israel, and Christianity. Except for the Story of the Cosmos, each evolved within the preceding stories. And each story has its own inner momentum, narrative, and cast of characters - which leads us to an important truth. Borrowing from Ojibway tradition, we may say that this succession constitutes a 'hierarchy of dependencies'.

In "Returning to the Teachings", Rupert Ross reports that

> the Ojibway hierarchy of Creation . . . is based on dependencies. It places the Mother Earth (and her lifeblood, the waters) in first place, for without them there would be no plant, animal or human life. The plant world stands second, for without it there would be no animal life. The animal world is third. Last, and clearly least important within this unique hierarchy, come humans. Nothing whatever depends on our survival.
>
> (65).

The succession of stories we have identified in this book is not a hierarchy of power or importance; it is one of inter-dependence. The dependence of Earth on the Cosmos is physical and biological; the dependence of humanity on Earth is physical and spiritual; the dependence of the Hebrews on humanity is primarily cultural; and the dependence of Christianity on the Hebrews is primarily religious. And, with the arrival of each new story, something unique enters the series.

Perhaps the most important lesson for contemporary people to draw from this hierarchy of dependence is to realize our complete dependence on the abundance of Earth's gifts; and, for those people who are faith seekers, to see Earth as a gift of a divine Creator.

GIFTS FROM EARTH AND HER MANY CREATURES

Western industrial society has for several centuries, and with increasing vigour, exercised human powers over nature, extracting materials from Earth with unprecedented technological skill to supply our needs and wants. During this same time Aboriginal societies have continued their ancient spiritual path of accepting gratefully from Earth and her creatures the gifts which they offer. Though Aboriginal Peoples have often been forced by incoming settlers to be secretive and cautious in practising their traditions, they have seldom entirely abandoned the wisdom of the elders. Moreover, in the last few decades we have seen a strong, creative movement among Aboriginals in many parts of the world which seeks to reclaim the heritage they were in danger of losing. Even among Westerners there is a dawning awareness that within the

116

Aboriginal heritage is wisdom and practice which can help to bring healing to many of the social and personal ills of modern technological society. Native traditions contain powerful teachings about how humans must receive Earth's bounty with conscious and explicit sensitivity and gratitude.

Aboriginal traditions emphasize attitudes of deep gratitude and profound dependence with respect to Earth and its creatures, attitudes others would do well to emulate. We will be rewarded by listening briefly to some of the elders' voices. Here are the opening lines of the book titled "The Sacred Tree":

> For all the people of the earth, the Creator has planted a Sacred Tree under which they may gather, and there find healing, power, wisdom and security. The roots of this tree spread deep into the body of Mother Earth. Its branches reach upward like hands praying to the Father Sky. The fruits of this tree are the good things the Creator has given to the people: teachings that show the path to love, compassion, generosity, patience, justice, courage, respect, humility and many other wonderful gifts.

Throughout the text of this book there are references to and lovely illustrations of animals with whom people share their life under the sacred Tree. Animals are teachers, sacred totems and life-givers, without whom humans cannot live well in this world and to whom they must give appropriate respect and thanks.

The centrality of animals in the Aboriginal world view is beautifully expressed in this creation story from the Iroquois and Huron Peoples.

> One day, down from the sky world a woman fell . . . two loons spread their wings together and formed a cushion to break her fall. . . . Great Turtle heard their wailing notes, and, gathering other creatures to him, came to the rescue.
>
> "My back is broad", he said. "Let me take her." Thus he relieved the loons of their heavy burden.
>
> As you know, Great Turtle, who now carries the world on his back, is endowed with many strange and wonderful powers. He knew that the woman and her offspring needed earth if they were to live. However, although Great Turtle has the power to make larger

117

whatever exists, he cannot create anything. Therefore, knowing that somewhere in the depths of the waters there was mud, he called on Beaver to dive to the bottom of the sea and bring some mud to the surface.

Beaver, realizing the depth he would be required to dive, at first objected. Then, urged on by Great Turtle, he agreed to try. Down he plunged; deeper and deeper he descended until he disappeared from the sight of Great Turtle and his companions, who were peering anxiously into the water. At first, bubbles of air broke its surface, but, after a few minutes, the undisturbed expanse gave no indication of life.

Just as they had given up hope, the almost lifeless form of Beaver rose to the surface. He had risked his life to carry out the wishes of Great Turtle, but without success. His paws gave no evidence of the slightest particle of mud.

Next Great Turtle sent Muskrat in search of mud. He also could find no end to the waters. Then Toad asked if he could try. Great Turtle refused. He was sure that, as Beaver and Muskrat had failed, this small creature would have no chance. But Toad insisted, and, more in weariness than consent, Great Turtle relented. Joyfully, Toad dived into the waters, which almost immediately swallowed him up. Time dragged on. The bubbles had long since ceased to rise to the surface. The loons and Beaver, who had now recovered, looked at Great Turtle and shook their heads.

Despairing, they were about to turn away when they saw the limp body of Toad floating on the water some distance from where he had disappeared. Gently, they lifted him out and, behold, within his lifeless mouth, Great Turtle saw some mud. Sadly he handed this to the woman, who placed it carefully on the edge of a shell. Gradually it spread, unevenly in places, forming into dips and mounds which grew larger and larger until mountains and valleys were formed.

Soon the world took shape, and was ready for trees and plants and animals.

(J.Morgan,
"When the Morning Stars Sang Together", pp 7-9.)

Animals are the central actors in the story. Their mutual interdependence and their valour in providing the originating matter of Earth for human habitation testify to the importance of animals for human existence.   Thus Aboriginal peoples, who for millenia listened to storytellers recounting tales about the interaction between humans and animals, learned to be grateful for all the ways animals provide gifts for our living.

Other teachings are described by Rupert Ross in his book "Returning to the Teachings". Two of these speak about fundamental attitudes which humans must have towards the nonhuman.

> All things change. There are two kinds of change. The coming together of things and the coming apart of things. . . . we will never be able to understand everything well enough to fully appreciate, predict, control or rearrange all those changes with any degree of certainty. . . . the web of ever-changing inter-dependence is so complex and so dynamic that only an arrogant fool would presume to understand it . . . we must all approach the universe from within a posture of profound humility
>
> (68-9).

> Creation demonstrates, at its most fundamental levels, principles of mutualism, interdependence and symbiosis. At those levels, all aspects of the created order are essential to the continued survival of Creation as a whole. According to that perspective, the obligation of humans is not to attack, insult or diminish them or each other, but to demonstrate respect, to offer support, to work towards compassion
>
> (78).

Ross stresses that the teachings emphasize the interdependence of everything which exists within and belongs to Earth. The teachings insist that wonder and respect are fundamental values essential for human survival. When we live this way, Earth becomes a vast cornucopia of gifts to be received with humble gratitude. In truth, Earth must be seen as foundational to the human, offering her gifts to meet our every need. Humans are utterly dependent on the bounty of Earth in order to survive.

These teachings reverse the normative cultural values of industrial society and reveal that a great many of our present ascendant social and economic priorities are death-dealing.   Our extractive economies advance their search for profits heedless of the enormous and mounting costs inflicted on land and sea and air, and on countless species being exterminated at an alarming rate. To correct this, we must replace our reckless and continuous demands placed upon Earth by an attitude of humble gratitude for gifts received.

In our urbanized societies we need a new sense of Earth as sacred, just as in our religious practice we need a renewed awareness of Sacred Presence. When we fail to recognize with thanksgiving the generosity of the Giver in providing for our needs, we act in the foolish presumption that everything in Earth is ours by right. Traditional Western religious convictions and actions need revising in the light of central teachings in Native culture. We find there that the generosity of the Creator is acknowledged constantly and gifts of the Great Spirit are deeply respected.

Nature is not a collection of objects but a communion of subjects. As we learn to live intentionally within this sacred communion, as subjects deeply interconnected with myriad other subjects, we shall understand that Earth is sacred. Earth is indeed a complex interconnection of material substances and living species, permeated and sustained by Sacred Presence which is at the heart of the universe. When we reflect this truth within our communal practices, such as eco-foresty, organic agriculture, and habitat protection, we are challenging our inherited attitude towards Earth as a collection of objects. We feel then the urgency to re-examine our attitudes and values. And in this process the teachings of Native wisdom are a strong ally. They can help us to be aware that we are totally dependent upon Earth not only for our material existence but also for the spiritual wisdom of Sacred Presence which orders everything on Earth.

LEARNING TO RECEIVE

In whatever way we may hear it, "I am generous" is the first Word which the Holy One addresses to humanity. This Word receives ample testimony and support from the magnificent cosmos in which we have a part - and especially from Earth, our island home. Aboriginal cultures bear important witness to this truth. The Christian church, however, has for centuries given more attention to humanity's duty to God and in consequence has failed to give adequate attention to the divine generosity.

A 19th-century spiritual teacher wrote to a friend:

> Our Lord gives to give and not to receive; very little suffices Him. Therefore accept everything from Him, however unworthy, however ungrateful, however 'unrepaying' you may be. Receive again and again. Rejoice in receiving, without after-thought. Ask again and again, and if possible, for ever more and more. Think always of that which you receive, never of that which you give. This is a far better way of entering into the love of our Lord and acquiring a boundless confidence in Him, than by looking at yourself and thinking of what you can do for Him.
>
> (Abbé de Tourville, "Letters of Direction", 68)

The Abbé infers that Christian people habitually think first of what they believe God requires of them; and this belief, he contends, has been sadly mistaken. The theme of obeying God, of doing the will of God, has been so strong in church training that it has almost eclipsed the first Word about God's generosity.

A basic error in church teaching has been to present the Holy One of biblical faith as an autocratic and demanding lawgiver. For example: Christians habitually misunderstand the true significance of the Ten Commandments. A typical recital of the Decalogue which is common in Christian catechetics and liturgy begins: "God said, you shall have no other gods before me. You shall not make ...." etc. etc. The Ten Commandments are heard as God's unqualified demands; they stand in solitary splendour as a divine imperative laid upon ancient Israel and upon us. But this is not correct. We hear the Decalogue in this mistaken way because the preceding and absolutely essential verse, Exodus 20:2, is almost always omitted: "I am the Lord your God, who brought you out of the land of Egypt, out of the house of slavery". Before there were divine commandments, there was the divine generosity. Before there was a developed Hebrew religion with its moral requirements, ancient Israel had known herself to be blessed by Yahweh, her God.

Before God asks, God gives.

Our need for a primary awareness of the divine initiative on behalf of

121

humanity's well-being is needed as urgently today as it was in the time of the ancient Hebrews. Nothing else can compare in importance with this as the original Good News of the Bible. And, as though to emphasize this truth, Israel was frequently charged by her prophets and sages with the sin of forgetting the mighty acts of God done on her behalf, of being ungrateful.

The strong, implied connecting word between the good news of God's generosity and the requirements laid upon Israel is THEREFORE. "I have given; THEREFORE I expect you to do these things." A wonderful, dramatic picture of this sequence - worth turning up and reading carefully - is found in Joshua Chapter 24, where the people are gathered for a ceremony of covenant renewal. But shorter forms of the same ritual of grateful remembering and faithful response, some only a few verses in length, are found in abundance throughout the Hebrew Scriptures.

A clear example is found in a text of Deuteronomy. Hebrew families are instructed to go to the local shrine of Yahweh with a basket of the first fruits of the harvest:

> When the priest takes the basket from your hand and sets it down before the altar of the Lord your God, you shall make this response before the Lord your God: "A wandering Aramean was my ancestor; he went down to Egypt and lived there as an alien . . . When the Egyptians treated us harshly and afflicted us, by imposing hard labor on us, we cried to the Lord, the God of our ancestors; the Lord heard our voice and saw our affliction, our toil, and our oppression. The Lord brought us out of Egypt with a mighty hand . . . and he brought us into this land, a land flowing with milk and honey. So now I bring the first fruit of the ground that you, O Lord, have given me".
>
> (26:1 ff)

In this ancient, simple and beautiful liturgy we see the correct ordering of Israel's faith and life. First, there is a recalling and recital in thanksgiving of the Lord's generosity in mighty acts; then follows the great THEREFORE of covenant faith, "So now . . ." Only then can the meaning of the gifts in the basket be understood.

As another example, listen to a psalmist ringing the changes on the great theme:

> I heard a voice I had not known:
> "I relieved your shoulder of the burden;
>> your hands were freed from the basket.
> In distress you called, and I rescued you;
>> I answered you in the secret place of thunder;
>> I tested you at the waters of Meribah. . . .
> I am the Lord your God,
>> who brought you up out of the land of Egypt.
> Open your mouth wide and I will fill it."
>
> (Psalm 81:5b-7,10)

> *I relieved, I rescued, I answered, I tested, I am .....*
> *Open your mouth wide and I will fill it!*

The central claim of biblical faith is that gifts of God are being continually offered to humanity, in expectation that we will want to learn how to be faithful to God's good purposes.

This traditional recital is primary in spite of the fact that in both Judaism and Christianity there are secondary traditions which insist that God's blessing must be earned by righteous living and will be lost through sin. Both Jew and Christian succumbed to the proud tendency to believe that we can and must earn God's blessing. The Bible, however, often speaks with more than one voice and we must learn to distinguish which voices are central for us now and which are only of historical interest. Though to make this distinction is not always a simple task, to be aware of its importance is a necessary first step.

It is evident in history that humanity has not always received as a precious gift all that we are offered for daily life. Human greed and short-sighted exploitation of nature's bounty have blinded humanity to the gratuitous Source of the amazing plethora of riches we have been given without our ever having to ask for them. Moreover, these gifts have never been withheld in spite of our ungrateful abuse of them. The biblical revelation teaches that the Holy One is not an 'enforcer' but is One who in love, sorrow and patience endures our willfulness. No act of God revokes the gifts in spite of our refusal to honour them - though Nature has her own ways of rebuking our foolishness and insolence.

The divine generosity is manifested to us first within Earth so that, as we recognize and accept these material blessings, we shall open our lives more deliberately to receive spiritual blessings as well. The Holy One yearns to supply everything needed for human physical and spiritual well-being and for the concomitant well-being of Earth. When we engage deeply with this truth - the priority of receiving gratefully even as we seek to respond faithfully - then traditional Christian approaches both to corporate worship and to personal devotions will be seen to require profound reform.

JUSTICE DENIED MEANS GENEROSITY SCORNED

> The Lord rises to argue his case;
>   he stands to judge the peoples.
> The Lord enters into judgment
>   with the elders and princes of his people:
> It is you who have devoured the vineyard;
>   the spoil of the poor is in your houses.
> What do you mean by crushing my people,
>   by grinding the face of the poor?
>   says the Lord of Hosts.
>
> (Isaiah 3:13-15)

> Jesus looked around and said to his disciples, "How hard it will be for those who have wealth to enter the Kingdom of God."
>
> (Mark 10:23)

Whether it is the world of Isaiah or of Jesus of Nazareth or of today, we see the wealth of Earth being denied to a substantial portion of humankind. Since the dawn of urban life, there have been few societies which ensured that over the span of generations there were no destitute people among them, no unjust distribution of wealth. During most of recorded human history, a minority of the population has manipulated economic affairs so as to become wealthy themselves and to leave others with too little. And in the last two decades the gap between rich and poor, both within and among nations, has been growing at an alarming rate. The human race, for whom Earth spreads out her bounty in such abundance, has treated material wealth as the preserve of a minority of people.

When the divine generosity is scorned in this way, it is difficult for

124

those who are poor to see that generosity or to believe in it. The unjust distribution of Earth's bounty means that the divine generosity is made invisible to a great many people.

In the biblical tradition there is vigorous condemnation of this state of affairs. Oracles of the prophets of ancient Israel, echoed in the words and works of Jesus, announce that the Holy One is righteous and requires the people of Earth to distribute material wealth so that justice is done. Not even pious observance of religious duties by the wealthy classes brings exemption from prophetic censure. Yahweh speaks through his servant Amos:

> Take away from me the noise of your songs;
>   I will not listen to the melody of your harps.
> But let justice roll down like water
>   and righteousness like an everflowing stream.
> (Amos 5:23-24)

Human society has failed constantly "to do justice and to love mercy." The divine generosity is mocked by human tolerance of social and economic injustice. Christians who speak of the wonder of the divine generosity in Nature's bounty are obliged by their own words to labour against injustices which distribute great wealth to the few and leave many without adequate provision for a decent life. People who talk about the generosity of God and fail to practise justice in social and economic life become an offense to the poor and to God.

Let us understand also that personal generosity to those in need fails to address society's radical disorder. The unequal distribution of wealth within any economic system is the result of skewed relationships built into that system. This being so, personal generosity can only be a source of very temporary respite for the poor. Unjust economic systems cannot be corrected by personal deeds of kindness. Only a changed social and economic order can bring society to an honest gratitude for the divine generosity. Until then all feelings of gratitude are tarnished by our tolerance of injustice.

The divine generosity is not necesarily a self-evident truth. The generosity which is embedded in the cosmos, and which for us is expressed most wondrously in Earth, must be translated into social and economic relations which are just and equitable, if all humanity is to be able to celebrate it. This is Good News which still waits to be lived throughout the length and breadth of the planet.

CHAPTER SUMMARY

The continuing generosity of the primal, creating Sacred Presence has always been evident to humanity in the abundance of Earth and of all her creatures. Traditional aboriginal teachings emphasize this. However, humanity's sense of gratitude and care for Earth has been seriously eroded in recent centuries. Our habitual abuse of Earth's gifts must now be halted; we must learn to live in harmony with the natural order.

Echoing this ancient wisdom, the first and basic claim of the Bible is that God is generous, wondrously and continuously generous. Israel declared this in her stories about escape from slavery in Egypt and entrance into a good land, and denied it in her national forgetfulness. Centuries later the first Christians learned about the divine generosity from Jesus, who warned against human tendencies to decline generous living and to seek wealth for oneself at the expense of others. If the Christian church is to heed his teaching, we have much work to do in creating social and economic justice.

The challenge, then as now, is to be willing to receive the abundant gifts of the generous God for the purposes for which they are given, knowing that we can only honour them if we are ready to use them as God intends. The well-being of Earth depends now upon humanity learning to live responsibly . And the first imperative is to develop a social and economic order which will promote compassion, justice and peace for all Earth's creatures.

AGENDA FOR CHRISTIANS

I will put my law within them, and I will write it on their
hearts; and I will be their God, and they shall be my
people. No longer shall they teach one another, or say to
each other, "Know the Lord", for they shall all know me,
from the least of them to the greatest, says the Lord.

Jeremiah 31:33-34

TRANSFORMING WORSHIP

Since its beginnings, the church has called faithful people to times of
worship in which they offer to the Holy One many things: praise,
thanksgiving, confession, intercession, material wealth. The image of
God which has validated this activity came to the church originally from
religious practice common throughout the ancient Near East. The gods
were believed to demand tribute for the same reasons that temporal lords
demanded it: they held absolute power. Just as it was the duty of subject
peoples to bring to temporal lords the tribute they demanded, so also it
seemed natural that the eternal Lord must be worshipped (offered worth-
ship) with appropriate offerings.

In religious mythology the heavenly realms and the life of the gods
were pictured as replicas of the royal courts on the earth. Details of
courtly behaviour present in local monarchical establishments were
heightened and given extravagant replication so that heavenly realms
became fabulous reproductions of temporal courts. Whatever was done
on earth to honour royalty was copied and heightened when earthlings
made tribute to the gods. Wherever heavenly power was acknowledged,
offerings were believed to be necessary to gain favours and to avoid
displeasure. In the courts of Egypt, for example, tribute was paid to
royalty in the form of agricultural and animal produce. Therefore, in the
temples of the Egyptian gods and goddesses sacrificial offerings were
made of grain and animals. And in ancient Israel the worship of Yahweh
echoed this pattern of Near Eastern religious cult and lore.

The dynamics of this relationship - between earthly religious practice and social custom on the one hand, and cultic expression of religious belief on the other - also operated in a reverse direction. Not only were heavenly abodes of the gods seen to be stylized copies of earthly royal establishments, but social and political relationships which favoured courtly elites were understood to be sanctioned by the gods. In this way heaven and earth were linked in a reciprocity of mutual benefit. The gods were seen as giving their blessing to the current social and political patterns in recognition of the worship being given to them. Thus, concerning the Babylonian creation story, Walter Wink observes ("Engaging the Powers", 16):

> The gods favor those who conquer. Conversely, whoever conquers must have the favor of the gods. The mass of people exists to perpetuate the power and privilege which the gods have conferred upon the king, the aristocracy, and the priesthood. Religion exists to legitimate power and privilege.

In Israel, the national cult lifted up Yahweh as the Eternal King. Conversely, Yahweh was believed to have established the temporal kingship of David and to guarantee the continuation of his dynasty. In Psalm 89, Yahweh speaks:

> I have found my servant David;
> > with my holy oil I have anointed him;
> my hand shall always remain with him;
> > my arm shall also strengthen him.
> The enemy shall not outwit him, the wicked shall not
> > humble him.
> I will crush his foes before him
> > and strike down those who hate him.
> My faithfulness and steadfast love shall be with him;
> > and in my name his horn shall be exalted. . . .
> I will establish his line forever,
> > and his throne as long as the heavens endure.
> > > > > > (Psalm 89:24-5, 29)

In passing, it is worth noting that this convenient partnership between the gods and kingly courts was frequently challenged in Israel by prophets of Yahweh. The immorality of the court and its minions brought upon them sharp criticism from Yahweh's prophets. In many biblical texts we see these prophets attacking the fork-tongued 'court' prophets who depended on royal patronage for their living, and in return provided the king with favourable oracles. Scribes of the Hebrew scriptures narrate these encounters with relish and sometimes with a delightful touch of sarcasm and humour, as in the story of Micaiah in 1 Kings 22:1-28.

In the religions of the ancient Near East, including the cult of Yahwism in Israel, descriptions of the gods - their moods, actions and demands - drew heavily upon what went on in royal courts. This was less true in Israel after Hebrew society no longer had monarchy, and when greater attention was being paid to the theme of covenant love between Yahweh and Israel. Nevertheless, the practice of sacrificial worship of Yahweh, with its hierarchical associations, retained a strong and enduring hold on Judahite imagination and practice until the destruction of the temple in 70 CE.

The Christian church inherited from the Jews, and from Near Eastern religion generally, this legacy of worship and religious practice together with much of the theology in which it was embedded. It is not surprising, then, that language relating to royalty was and still is prominent in Christian liturgies. The Christian God is addressed as King and Lord, who reigns in majesty and power. And this symbolism has had enormous influence on the minds and hearts of Christian people since the time of the church's beginnings. To this day, church worship carries a strong emphasis on praise, thanksgiving, petition and offerings made to the divine King of the Universe.

This traditional Christian understanding of worship is dramatically illustrated in the New Testament writing, "The Revelation to John", as for example in 4: 9,11:

> And whenever the living creatures give glory and honour and thanks to the one who is seated on the throne, who lives for ever and ever. . . they cast their crowns before the throne, singing,
>> "You are worthy, our Lord and God,
>> to receive glory and honour and power,
>> for you created all things,
>> and by your will they existed and were created."

The text extols the glory, honor and power ascribed to God by the heavenly host. But if we listen carefully we can hear in this hymn an echo (suitably modified) of words being addressed to an enthroned monarch in some ancient Near Eastern royal court, and to some traditional deity ensconced in heavenly mansions.

In this enduring and rich tradition of deference and honour towards royalty and the gods lies one of the major roots of the dominant tradition in Christianity today. All the images of the majesty and power of the enthroned Eternal King, the God and Father of the Lord Jesus Christ, come in a direct line from that ancient religious practice.

This imagery and this cultic practice, however, are losing legitimacy in the minds and hearts of contemporary people. Images of God drawn from hierarchical court life become dysfunctional as increasing numbers of people reject absolute monarchy and authoritarian political rule in society. Speech about 'Almighty God' and the 'Lordship' of Christ draws upon obsolete imagery. 'Glory talk' relating to the Eternal Christ obscures Jesus as the man of Nazareth, as a servant prophet among his people. It contradicts our convictions about him as "the man for others". Glory talk makes us deaf to vital biblical teaching about Jesus' lowliness and about the daily companionship the Holy One offers us in our life journey.

An insistent question appears as we review these matters. When images of the Holy One are stripped of the trappings of royalty and dominion, what remains in the notion of 'worshipping God'? When central religious symbols change so that they no longer speak about a God who needs to receive human offerings, but speak rather about a divine passion to be generous in response to human need - what is left of the notion of prayer and praise offered to God? If symbols of the Holy One become less about power and more about a mystery of lowliness and the divine generosity, *what happens to worship*?

A further question: as the new cosmology leads us to a sense of Sacred Presence throughout the universe, to a sense of the divine immanence in creation, to a recognition that Earth is a Matrix of the Divine - how does this change the manner in which we understand our relationship to the Holy One?

And this conclusion. If in the future the Christian religion is to engage human minds and hearts with liberating and transforming power, we must discover new language and new actions for public liturgies which can express a new understanding of what is meant by 'God'.

Fortunately, in the search for new liturgies which depart from traditional notions of worship, we have solid ground on which to build. This ground can be found first and foremost in our present practice of community recital. In our liturgical gatherings we regularly recount the historic acts of divine grace drawn from the biblical narrative: we remember and celebrate all that the Holy One did through the ancient Hebrews and in Jesus of Nazareth. We tell our sacred stories derived from the biblical literature. And now we must expand our use of community recital to articulate the amazing reality of the natural order in which we are embedded, and to celebrate humanity's part in the unfolding stories of Earth and of the universe. We can learn to tell about our experiences of Sacred Presence within the cosmic reality, whether that be in the microcosm or macrocosm.

The continuing imperative for a Christian community to be together before their God arises from the struggles and victories, the sorrows and joys, which we experience in daily living. We come together to give thanks for God's gifts in days gone by and to seek spiritual gifts for tasks ahead. We gather to celebrate achievements in the struggles for justice, peace and communal well-being. Whenever people give themselves in loving care for others; whenever they act to challenge forces of destruction in society; whenever they gently and imaginatively steward the Earth and its creatures - there God's truth and purpose are being served. And all of this needs to be celebrated in our liturgies.

It is equally necessary for people to gather for community lamentation. In a radically disordered world, our attempts to live creatively often bring discouragement, spiritual fatigue and suffering. We need liturgies where we share our grief for society and for Earth, where we seek healing and renewal. We come together in the presence of the Holy One as tired pilgrims who have attempted to be faithful to the ways of compassion and justice in a confused and broken world. We have mistakes to confess and wounds to be healed; we have minds and spirits needing to be inspired. We want to meet with the God whose giving is foolishly generous by human standards, to be with the God who waits to use us in making all things new.

In none of this is there any need to ask what is 'due to God' beyond our continuing attempts to live in faithful love to the Creator and to creatures. What needs to flow from our hearts is thanksgiving for divine blessings.

> Happy are those whose help is the God of Jacob,
>   whose hope is in the Lord their God,
> who made heaven and earth,
>   the sea, and all that is in them;
> who keeps faith forever;
>   who executes justice for the oppressed;
>   who gives food to the hungry.
> The Lord sets prisoners free;
>   and the Lord opens the eyes of the blind.
> The Lord lifts up those who are bowed down
>   the Lord loves the righteous.
>
> (Psalm 146:6 - 8)

It is the mood of the psalmist that we must note. His preoccupation is with the eternal generosity of Yahweh. Israel's task was to learn that she must accept all she was offered by Yahweh in order to be able to live with compassion and justice. The Holy One seeks nothing else from us other than this faithfulness - and a deep interior loving which desires to respond to the active divine loving.

And one final comment. In our communal liturgies we must name the reality of our daily living much more explicitly than has been customary. The present familiar pattern of comfortable generalizations in public worship often makes our liturgies banal and causes our prayer to drift away from the concrete realities of our lives. The Hebrew psalmists have much to teach us about being explicit when sharing our joys and sorrows, our needs and our interior wounds. The Book of Psalms is replete with the specifics of its own times, with the concrete realities of Hebrew life. We will be able to bring daily life into our communal gatherings only if we are specific, flexible and imaginative in our language, and ready to experiment in liturgical song and body movement.

The rejuvenation of our faith practice in the celebration of God's presence among us is joyful work. The much needed renewal in liturgy must draw upon the wisdom, imagination and enthusiasm of everyone. We shall continue to require the resources of specialists, of theologians and liturgists; but the work of renewal also needs the constant input of the people who are doing the liturgy together. If liturgy is to be an expression of the faith of a community, then that community needs to be constantly recreating their 'public work' (which is the literal meaning of the Greek word for 'liturgy'). Excellent examples of this approach to public prayer come from the "Asian Women's Resource Centre for Culture and Theology." In the "Liturgical Sample" in Appendix 'B', I reproduce a few excerpts from their literature.

- o - o - o - o - o -

There are some obvious challenges ahead in accomplishing a transformation of the liturgical practice of the church. Some of these challenges come from the heavy emphasis in Western Christianity on human sin and the threatened punishment for sin. For example, there is no place in a renewed liturgical practice for language which implies that it is necessary to beg mercy from God. The well-known liturgical refrain Kyrie eleison, "Lord have mercy", makes a false statement about our relationship to the Holy One. We do not need to ask for mercy. On the contrary, 'loving kindness' is one of the ways in which the Hebrews named the Holy One, and Jesus of Nazareth exemplified this quality. God is the Merciful One and mercy is one of the assured ways in which God companions humanity. Mercy is not something for which we need to ask, even though we have much to learn about what it actually means, how we shall accept it, and how we shall live by it.

There are indeed times when alienated hearts may cry out to their God, desiring to know the healing grace of forgiveness. But in doing this, we shall remember that God is always present to us in persistent divine healing love, waiting for the beloved to accept what is being offered. We do not need to sing "Kyrie eleison". But we do need the practice of contrition in a new moral earnestness. We must face up honestly and deliberately to the fact of sin, both personal and social, searching out what spiritual and moral transformation mean in practice. Spiritual growth does not come by way of "cheap grace" (Dietrich Bonhoeffer's phrase) begged from God. It comes from clarity about our own lives, which in turn comes from moral enlightenment nurtured within a believing community.

A second and related example of an obstacle to liturgical reform is the refrain, "Lord, I am not worthy". This phrase, taken from a gospel scene, occurs sometimes in formal prayers and litanies. It worries about something which does not worry God. Worthiness is not an issue between God and the human. Worthy of what? Presumably of God's friendship. But it is precisely this ready divine friendship which is evident in many of the Hebrew psalms and in the life and teachings of Jesus. Christian faith affirms that we are loved as we are, and this is true even when we decline to accept and live in the strength of that loving.

A third example of liturgical and devotional language which needs clarification is "God forgive us." Since there is no doubt that God is forgiving, it is more truthful to say, "Our God, we rejoice in your forgiving love and gladly receive it." Can we find ways of bringing our wounded spiritual state into the divine Presence with feelings of sorrow completed by gratitude, celebrating the love which is already ours? That is what we need to do. Prayers of true repentance bring feelings of joy, not doubts about how we shall access God's gift of healing love.

Basic to repentance is trust in God; but trust in God matures only slowly and needs the constant encouragement of remembering that the divine forgiveness is unwavering. It may seem paradoxical, but if we are to venture into the unmarked and demanding route of moral transformation, we need to know that we have forgiveness for sins even before we commit them. It cannot be said too often - the Holy One accepts the trial and error of our living and brings the divine forgiveness and healing to our repentance. Contrition for moral failure rooted in the knowledge of God's love is a highroad to friendship with God. It is moral indifference and moral complacency which block the way and leave God's wondrous forgiving love unnoticed and unaccepted.

One necessary qualification to these comments is present in the prayer that Jesus gave to disciples (Luke 11:1ff): "forgive us our sins, for we ourselves forgive everyone indebted to us." As we learn to forgive others we shall be more open to the forgiveness which is always there in

134

God for us. But if we harden our hearts against the faults of others, we shall not be able to appreciate or accept what forgiveness means for our own faults.

We need also to balance our prayers of confession with prayers for interior healing. All people carry soul wounds which are often much more debilitating than are their sinful acts. We are crippled by undesirable twists of character received in the early years of life, deformations for which we bear no personal responsibility even though as adults we may learn to accept responsibility for their consequences. These are 'interior wounds', sometimes expressed as lying, cheating, sarcasm, dominating others, hurting those close to us, etc. Injuries to ourselves and to others which come from this 'acting out' of our interior wounds usually far outstrip injuries resulting from deliberate moral faults. The fallout from behaviour caused by interior wounds is at least as damaging in human relationships as are the consequences of sins. Culpable sin is present *only when we consciously decide* to act against a moral standard which we have accepted as binding for ourselves. Culpable sin calls for repentance; interior wounds wait to be healed.

It is instructive to note that in the gospel stories we see Jesus responding in compassion to people's broken lives much more often than we see him troubled by their sins. Why, then, does the church repeatedly accent our sins and say almost nothing about these deep, interior wounds? In the future, our liturgies must give as much attention to our need for spiritual healing as to our need to know moral faults and to accept forgiveness.

And what shall we say about intercessory prayer, prayer for the needs of other people? If we believe in a loving and discerning God, who knows and is addressing our concerns even before we name them, what does it mean to ask for God's help? When we drop the presumption of divine omnipotence - that God is able to answer our prayers by some kind of divine intervention - much content of traditional intercessory prayer changes. Strange as it may seem, God waits for our permission and our cooperation before acting in and through us to transform our world to the ways of compassion, justice and peace. We need to replace our intercessions with prayers which desire the free run of the Spirit in us,

135

which welcome the One who will enable our care for one another and for Earth, which open us to the mystery of love acting through us. Anglican Archbishop William Temple wrote, "Honest prayer begins with a willingness to be identified with the answer."

To complete these observation about changes to public liturgy we must recall traditional attribution of male gender to the Divine. God is unequivocally HE in both Hebrew and Christian Scriptures. This is not surprising since the culture of the ancient Near East at that time was securely patriarchal (which explains why Jesus called God, "Abba", Daddy). However, we cannot continue with this practice, nor can we attribute female gender to God. We may well continue, for a time at least, to speak of God as mother-like and father-like, using that language analogically to image some of God's ways with us. But the Holy One is neither Father nor Mother; we must discover ways in which to name Sacred Presence without assigning gender.

A very familiar liturgical text says, "Lamb of God, you take away the sin of the world; have mercy upon us". For reasons historical, biblical and theological we must discard this ancient text and the teaching based upon it. But in making this change the church faces a complex situation. Both liturgy and hymnology make extensive use of atonement teaching. References abound to Jesus as the bearer of human sin, to Jesus as the perfect Sacrifice, as the divine Mediator. On the other hand, there are several powerful solvents at work in church and society which, whether we want it or not, will gradually remove this teaching from Christianity.

First, much contemporary Christian scholarship is abandoning the classical Doctrine of the Atonement. In chapter three I cited only six authors, but many other writers in various schools of Creation and Liberation theology are denying or ignoring this teaching. It will die of neglect when it is not being deliberately rejected. I give the final word here on this subject to Walter Wink:

> The God whom Jesus revealed as no longer our rival, no longer threatening and vengeful, but unconditionally loving and forgiving, who needed no satisfaction by blood - this God of infinite mercy was metamorphosed by the church into the image of a God whose demand for blood atonement leads to God's requiring of his own Son

a death on behalf of us all. The nonviolent God of Jesus comes to be depicted as a God of unequaled violence, since God not only allegedly demands the blood of the victim who is closest and most precious to him, but also holds the whole of humanity accountable for a death that God both anticipated and required. Against such an image of God the revolt of atheism is an act of pure religion.

("Engaging the Powers", 149)

There is no longer any place for atonement theology in our liturgies.

Second, a check with Christian friends who no longer are connected to any church reveals how little importance is attached by many of them to teaching about atonement. People separated from the church but still open to the Christian religion are looking for other explanations of Jesus' life and death. *Vox populi* is not always *vox dei*, but in this case it is.

A third solvent of this doctrine comes from Christians of serious ethical commitment. These folk realize how much humanity is itself responsible to bring healing and hope to the world. Consider these words of Dietrich Bonhoeffer:

> The difference between the Christian hope of resurrection and a mythological hope is that the Christian hope sends a man*(sic) ba*ck to his life on earth in a wholly new way . . . . Myths of salvation arise from human experiences of the boundary situation. Christ takes hold of a man at the centre of his life.

("Letters and Papers from Prison", 112-113)

Church teaching about eternal salvation is a "boundary situation" which has generated all kinds of "mythological hope" (in the pejorative use of that term). Bonhoeffer emphasizes the need to turn from this hazy mirage on our spiritual horizons and to assume full responsibility for our life now. In his letters he insists on this point by speaking frequently of "the adulthood of the world", "the world come of age". Bonhoeffer is troubled by Christian tendencies to look to God to solve the problems of life on earth, problems which he considers God has assigned to us: "We should find God in what we do know, not in what we don't; not in outstanding problems, but in those we have already solved" (*ibid*, 104). It is a mistake to look to Jesus as the single source of the world's salvation.

The question of human responsibility for the future of Earth is precisely where, in its practical implications, the classical Doctrine of the Atonement finally collapses. Jesus does not save us from the folly of our ways. The evidence has been accumulating for centuries. Either with God's generous guidance and grace we ourselves will deal with the bitter fruit of human sin, or we shall destroy Earth as a place of human habitation. It may be a daunting task to remove atonement theology from the church's liturgy and hymnody but we don't have a choice. With consideration and care, it can and must be done.

Our departure from atonement theology also has implications for the Christians' central liturgy. The Eucharist can no longer be seen as a commemoration of Jesus' sacrificial death for the salvation of the world. Rather, we must look for the central meaning of the Eucharist in Jesus' own apparent joy in sharing meals with people of the Galilean countryside. The open table of Jesus' public life challenged the discriminatory social code of honour and shame which denied the Jewish peasantry the right to share meals with members of other social classes. By embracing an open table, Jesus taught a seminal truth of the Reign of God: all people are to be included as equals in the community of God's people. The Eucharist can mean no less for us today.

Jesus' words over the bread and wine of his last meal with the inner circle of disciples, "this is my body . . . this is my blood of the new covenant", are symbolic. We can be reasonably sure that those early disciples understood the words to indicate they were sharing in resurrection life. The words are strong metaphors for the experience of receiving new life which flows from the risen Master.

The bread and wine of this sacred meal also carry clear reference to the roots of human life in vital Earth substances. Bread and wine were basic to the diet of Palestinian peasants and they are still strong symbols of our own connection to Earth. The Eucharist is a sacred meal about community among people and the inter-relatedness of all life.

The entire liturgy, in all its words and actions, must be rethought. What I have been suggesting about the sacredness of Earth, about images of the Holy One, and about our understanding of Jesus, must be reflected in the Eucharist.

The heart of liturgical renewal is this: in communal gatherings we need to transform our language, our visual images, our use of space and structure, our music and our body movement, so that we may become

> more aware of Sacred Presence
>
> more open to Sacred Presence
>
> more responsive to Sacred Presence.

Within renewed liturgical discourse and drama we must learn to name the hopes and joys and sorrows of a world where we are working to build compassion, justice and peace. Within this spiritual/political work, an on-going and central task is to discover names of the Holy One which have power to capture our imaginations and to stir our wills. We need people committed to generous living in the twenty-first century. But at present this work is inhibited by traditional ways of naming the Holy One. Our society flounders for lack of a dynamic fabric of meanings constructed around more truthful names for Sacred Presence.

Consider, for example, the following:

> Great Spirit, Sacred Mystery, Generous Love, Creative
> Wisdom, Sacred Cosmic Energy, Word of Truth,
> Soul Friend, Hidden Heart of the Cosmos, Light Within,
> Gentle Compassion, Immanent Spirit,
> Beloved Companion, Life of the soul

These names are but hints of the range of images that we must test to determine how well they help us to be aware of Sacred Presence. Religious poetry and drama are needed to open our souls to the Divine. Some names point into the vastness of the universe, some point to Earth and its creatures, some point to the human spirit, and some point in more than one way. But however we do it, the work of naming the Holy One appropriately is urgent so that we may become more aware of and open and responsive to Sacred Presence.

Have we the courage to risk new paths of the spirit? To sense the deep change of feeling which will be present within the shift in religious understanding, imagination, language and practice which I have outlined, picture two ways a child could approach a parent. The first picture shows the child being cautious and unsure, uncertain whether what is sought will be given, unclear about what must be done in order to please, wondering how to gauge the mood of the parent so as to make the right presentation of desire. A second picture shows the child making a wild rush into the parent's arms, jumping up to hug the older one, absolutely certain of a warm welcome from the adult who waits to bless the little one. This child is confident that what is sought and will be given is the best possible for the moment, though all the child's present desires may or may not be met. The first picture reflects a religious attitude which has gripped the human heart and imagination for millennia. The second picture reflects the changes we have been considering in these pages.

Before we leave this discussion about how in our communal gatherings we shall express our relationship to God, it is important to notice that there are significant ethical implications for the life of society at large in the changes I am advocating. When god language refers to an awe-inspiring Supreme Power, the religious duty of human beings becomes the offering of sacrifices, petitions, intercessions and humble gratitude to the deity. The flow of energy and duty is from humanity to God, even though we acknowledge (faintly, in the background) that God is the Creator from whom everything comes. We have been trained to call this our worship of God. And when this religious imagery is mirrored within social relationships in general, ideological support is given to a social order in which the strong are served by the weak. Human social relations develop in which a hierarchy of privilege is validated, with no prestige being assigned to the lowest classes and a large portion to the highest classes. How many societies have been structured with that social order in view! People endowed with plentiful personal talents and possessions are taught to feel that these are rights and privileges which may on occasion lead them to express to the lower classes an appropriate philanthropic *noblesse oblige*. This pattern of social relationships is by far the most common in human history, strengthened by what has been the dominant religious ideology.

On the other hand, when the image of the Holy One expresses companionship with and generosity towards humanity, the flow is reversed. Now we understand that the Holy One yearns constantly to give, and that we need to learn to receive with thanksgiving. When this religious imagery is mirrored into society, the stronger are encouraged and perhaps even inspired to serve the weaker. People with greater talents and possessions find in their circumstances a natural and wonderful opportunity to be generous and not condescending to those less fortunate. Indeed, in an ideal state, one could imagine a gentle and good-natured rivalry among persons most well endowed to see who could be the most generous to those in need. Any move toward the latter practice in social relationships would take a currently upside-down world and begin to place it on its feet.

A GREAT DIVIDE

Many changes in Christian thought and practice are needed if Christian faith and life are to take an active and creative role in the present momentous shift occuring within human spiritual awareness. Until relatively recent times, humanity's basic activities which provide food, clothing and shelter were frequently threatened with disaster by drought, floods, disease, wild animals, and other vicissitudes of nature. Life was uncertain for most people most of the time. In these circumstances, it is not surprising that religion developed a strong petitionary thrust which sought from the supernatural order the blessings of harvest, physical safety and natural reproduction.

This kind of religious practice has been declining rapidly during the last century. Most of humanity is already or soon will be free from any tendency to seek material needs and security from supernatural intervention. We are learning that we must look to ourselves in cooperation with the natural order for the provision of human needs as we reach for a just and sustainable life for all people and for Earth itself.

We stand astride one of the great divides in the human odyssey. For us, true religion can no longer be rooted in the ancient arts of courting the divine favour: pleading, interceding, petitioning, and making sacrificial offerings in order to catch the attention of the gods and to win their intervention for our interests. And though the great world religions have now almost dispensed with formal material offerings to the gods we have yet to leave behind the so-called spiritual sacrifices which find their justification in the same obsolete religious ideology.

We live in a time of transition which is exciting and rewarding, but difficult. This is a time of overlap between a radically new religious understanding and practice, and 'old time religion'. It will take our best efforts to manage this transition with care and understanding, sensitive to the intense feelings and convictions on both sides of the divide.

Whatever we shall mean by 'God' in the future must be consistent with two fundamental truths. First, humanity has responsibility for sensitive stewardship of human life and of the natural order which we share with other creatures. Second, we require spiritual vision and moral commitment to sustain and guide our stewardship of society and nature. These spiritual and moral resources come to us through the beauty and wonder of the natural order, through our general social relationships, through personal and communal response to Sacred Presence, and through the mediation of faith communities. In our attempts at responsible living, we are never alone.

A transformed religious understanding and practice are rooted in a transformed image of the Divine. When we truly believe in the over-flowing generosity of Sacred Presence, our religious practices shake off any suggestion of offerings to the Holy One and become the means of opening ourselves to receive wondrous gifts and of expressing our gratitude for them. All other ways in which we seek to be open to Sacred Presence follow from that central conviction.

To support this understanding, traditional Christian teaching pro-claims a paradox. We are called to believe in a generous God who, when we use the standards of worldly wisdom, seems foolish, and who, when we use worldly definitions of power, seems weak (1 Cor 1:22-25). With Paul the Apostle we see this truth most clearly in Jesus of Nazareth, a man transparent to the Divine who was willing to accept his own premature death as an expression of his profound love for humanity.

The Holy One does not need persuasion to act for human blessing and well-being. It is we who must renounce that interior 'turning away' which refuses God's generosity to us. This turning away of the human from the Divine is the most profound meaning of the word 'sin', a word prominent in Hebrew-Christian discourse. Sound religious practice must be grounded in a turning towards the divine goodwill and be expressed in responsible stewardship of all life on planet Earth.

PERSONAL PRAYER

There is another negative consequence which may follow from our lack of truthful images and symbols for the Holy One and for Jesus of Nazareth: personal prayer becomes awkward, difficult or empty. Indeed, problems in using traditional prayers are an early sign that the old teachings no longer work for us. If we have been people of prayer, our praying may stumble or die. If we are beginners, there seems to be nowhere in the traditional forms to begin a serious practice of prayer. We must find a new language of prayer and a new context for prayer in a changed understanding of our relationship with the Holy One.

The practice of prayer must be placed in a wide context. Religious faith and life walk on three 'legs' which are bound together in strong interdependence. First is the intellectual work of seeking to determine what it is we believe. That is the primary focus of this book. Second is moral endeavour, the daily effort "to do justice and to love kindness". The third leg is prayer, both personal and communal, the heart opening to God.

There are many means by which people seek to open themselves to the Holy One. From time immemorial humans have found their sense of Sacred Presence mediated by Nature, music, dance, architecture and the graphic arts. But here I am concerned only with personal prayer and particularly that which is discursive, linguistic. Cynical folk have sometimes suggested that this kind of prayer is merely auto suggestion, that there is no actual divine partner at all. That comment, of course, points to a basic challenge we face in trying to pray. We do need to wonder constantly who God is for us, and how we might name God according to our present religious understanding so that there can be true spiritual meeting between the self and the divine Other. We play with images, we experiment with language, we use silence, we try out different times and places in which to be present to Sacred Presence - if only to become more aware of Mystery beyond us and yet present to us. And this is not necessarily auto suggestion; this is truly an adventure in opening ourselves to the divine Other.

I have been stressing that God is generous and does not need to be summoned in order to be present. Since God yearns for us with a vulnerable desire, our prayer does not need to be clever, but honest. Since God does not stand over us in judgment but embraces us in love to disarm our fear, our prayer can be bold and experimental. We need not concern ourselves with taking wrong directions but only with how to keep trying.

All prayer must contain the intention and effort to open ourselves to divine generosity. Simone Weil calls this "an act of attention and consent". We will never find God; but since God is seeking us then we have good reason to search for new ways of opening our hearts to the Seeker. And we want to be found.

It has been customary in traditional prayer to use 'invocation', inviting the Spirit to be with us. But such prayer can also be seen as rejoicing in the ever present Paraclete (Advocate) who dwells within the soul, as in the following beautiful traditional prayer poem:

> Come Thou, Holy Paraclete, and from thy celestial seat
>   send thy light and brilliancy;
> Lover of the poor draw near, Giver of all gifts be here,
>   Come, the soul's true radiancy.
>
> Come, of comforters the best, of the soul the sweetest guest,
>   Come in toil refreshingly;
> Thou in labour rest most sweet, thou art shadow from the heat,
>   Comfort in adversity.
>
> O Thou light most pure and blest, shine within the inmost breast
>   of thy faithful company;
> where Thou art not, we have nought; every holy deed and thought
>   comes from thy divinity.
>
> What is soilèd make Thou pure, what is wounded work its cure,
>   what is parchèd, fructify;
> What is rigid gently bend; what is frozen warmly tend;
>   strengthen what goes erringly.
>
> Fill thy faithful who confide in thy power to guard and
>   guide with the sevenfold mystery;
> here thy grace and virtue send, grant salvation in the end
>   and in heaven felicity.

The Holy One is always present to us, but sometimes we have difficulty being present to the Holy One. It is we who become absent, out of touch - but not God. The language of prayer must be designed to help us recognize this truth and help us to be open to Sacred Presence.

In prayer we struggle to name the Holy One in ways which ring authentically in our minds and hearts. We also work to discover self-knowledge which is truthful, which names the person we are now with as much accuracy and honesty as possible. As we increase in truthful self-knowledge we increase our ability to be present to Sacred Presence. Classical spiritual teaching urges us to practice daily self-examination and to come before the Holy One "with a humble and contrite heart".

Authentic prayer is shaped by how we answer two questions: Who are You for me now? Who am I for You now? When the mystery of the human soul reaches to touch the holy darkness of Sacred Presence, these questions often receive unexpected answers, giving us insights which change how we pray. Within the limitations of our human awareness and understanding, in prayer which is open-ended and vital, neither the human person nor the divine Other is a stable reality; both are dynamic, fluid and evolving.

Evelyn Underhill, writing in "The Golden Sequence", says:

> It is the special function of prayer to turn the self away from the time-series, and towards adoration and adherence. Prayer opens the doors of the psyche to the invasion of another order, which shall at its full term transform the very quality of our existence.

(p.3)

There are many avenues into this work. We can try revising traditional prayers which we have previously found helpful. That is, we can change familiar words to match our present needs and understanding more adequately, to help us express more truthfully who we are now and how we name the Holy One. Or again, we may choose to develop our own prayers which open us to Sacred Presence. In these ways we experiment with new language of the soul. In this sacred dance of discovery between the human and the Divine, as we enter into a new inner integrity, prayer is truly happening. This is joyful work. We know then that there is a divine Companion who assists us in our personal growth and in our faithful living with others.

Personal prayer is dancing with an experienced Partner, not presenting requests to an enthroned monarch. Prayer is taking up with a sympathetic Friend an honest exploration of our feelings and thoughts about life; it is not apologizing to a remote deity for the person we are.

Personal prayer is a kind of sacred play in which we juggle images and symbols, thoughts and feelings, to break open our time-bound and space-bound hearts and welcome the Divine. Prayer is a means by which the Spirit teaches us who God is for us, who we are for God, and how we may carry out our responsibilities to other people and to Earth. In prayer we hold in love, and before the Holy One, those parts of life for which we have special concern. We name the brokenness of our world so that we ourselves may be strengthened to do the healing works of love. We desire to be partners with the active divine loving as it participates in the life of the world.

In the work of prayer we experiment with language, music, body movement and physical artifacts to create a landscape for the soul where we can open ourselves to the Beloved. Prayer is an adventure of turning ourselves toward Sacred Presence so that our understanding, our feelings and our desire become illuminated by Spirit. We welcome the gifts of God's generosity and are led more completely into our own true humanity. And perhaps, beyond all our sacred play, we will discover an unencumbered freedom of soul which is a response of pure joy to the Holy One. Call it adoration, a lover present to her or his Beloved, both to receive and to respond.

PRAYER AND PROTEST

Prayer, both personal and communal, can be a rewarding experience which contributes to spiritual insight and moral life. But the human journey is not always kind to us and external circumstances do not always support our best efforts to live creatively. Life does not necessarily bring spiritual consolation; frequently it brings desolation. In that context prayer has a different function, one which accords well with images of God developed in these pages.

In the concluding section of Chapter Five we considered three levels of suffering. Commenting on the first two, I wrote:

> Job, in the Hebrew writing of that name, resigned himself to the early catastrophes which overcame him even though they inflicted unimaginable misery and pain. There came a time, however, when his pain changed in character and he cursed God. Now he was overwhelmed with his sufferings because there was no longer any discernible meaning in what was happening to him. He experienced an unspeakable insult to his being.

The same depth of suffering is reflected in Psalm 88, and especially in the concluding verses where God is directly challenged:

> Your wrath has swept over me;
>   your dread assaults destroy me.
> They surround me like a flood all the day long;
>   from all sides they close in on me.
> You have caused friend and neighbour to shun me;
>   my companions are in darkness.

Such accusations by Israel against Yahweh are not uncommon in the Hebrew Scriptures. They point to a significant aspect of the nation's experience and must be seen in the context of the nation's troubled history. Several times ancient Israel experienced national destruction and despoliation of her homeland. At such times the people struggled to retain their covenant faith in Yahweh's good will towards them and in this struggle they learned to protest to Yahweh about their plight. In times of desperation and sorrow, they developed the form of prayer known as 'lament'. Walter Brueggemann observes:

> Lament-speech takes courage because it pushes the relationship [of Israel to Yahweh] to the boundaries of unacceptability. It takes risks because one does not know how the great God will receive it. It might have been an act of disobedience that would be crushed according to the normal rules of authority and propriety. It requires not only deep faith but new faith. It takes not only nerve but a fresh hunch about this God. The hunch is that this God does not want to be an unchallenged structure but one that can be frontally addressed. Such is the hope or yearning of lamenting Israel.
>
> ("Old Testament Theology", 28)

Such also is the hope and yearning of the Christian prayer of protest. Following the lead of ancient Israel, Christians can be bold in their speech to God in times of tribulation. We believe that we will be heard out and that our pain will be taken seriously. Indeed, Israel believed that the ways of the Holy One could change as a result of her lamentation, that the declared agony of God's people could open up new ways for the Holy One to act.

Confronting the Holy One with the deep sorrows of our hearts is an essential part of the journey of faith, though it involves courage and risk. Our questions, fears, bewilderment and suffering belong regularly and explicitly in the liturgies of the Christian community and in personal prayer. That this practice is seldom found in our churches is a telling comment on an inadequacy of both our theology and our piety. God can be trusted to respond to our deep sorrows; indeed, in times of distress our prayer of lamentation is essential for spiritual healing.

In a time of extreme distress in my own life, I went many times into a church building and hurled at the altar words which I had memorized from Psalm 51:

> Purge me with hyssop, and I shall be clean;
>   wash me, and I shall be whiter than snow.
> Let me hear joy and gladness,
>   let the bones which you have crushed rejoice.
> Hide your face from my sins,
>   and blot out all my iniquities.

Those words were able to carry some of the deepest pain and sorrow I had ever known. And I knew that they were received. The act of challenging God was one of my paths to healing.

In discussing this subject, Brueggemann shows how, in the practice of religious complaint, we experience not only personal healing but also learn how to participate in the healing of the body politic. Every human institution, social, economic, political and ecclesiastical, is in danger of becoming a structure which resists and resents challenge. The more powerful it becomes the more it refuses to be confronted. In pretensions to absolute authority it begins to claim "there is no alternative" to its governance, to practices which are being seen clearly by the community as faulty. Here, too, people of faith need to proclaim that life has gone wrong, that society is sick, that power is being used irresponsibly and unacceptably. God is not the only external authority which can be felt as intimidating and unresponsive. We can learn to be courageous as people of faith and confront 'the powers' by declaring our suffering and the suffering of others.

A vital lesson to be gained from our practice of forthright and honest prayers of lamentation is that we have the right and are capable of mustering the courage to bring our pain before established authority in all spheres of life. It is part of our human freedom and responsibility. Knowing that God desires an open and forthright relationship with us, we learn how to declare before the Holy One our negative feelings and thoughts, our personal and public pain. The same kind of readiness and courage for creative complaint and open challenge is necessary in our relationships with institutions holding power in our society. Such actions are essential for social, economic and political well-being. City Hall needs to hear our protest against unjust and inhuman policies and actions, City Hall needs to hear our pain. What we learn to do in prayer, both personal and communal, may well give us courage to seek the common good in public life. The practice of religion and the practice of politics are not so far apart as people sometimes suppose.

AFFIRMING THE INDWELLING SPIRIT

In all aspects of our life, in the works of heart and mind and hand, we can learn to depend upon the Holy One as "Indwelling Spirit". It is this traditional name of God which we need most to understand and use today. Evelyn Underhill is a pre-eminent teacher in this endeavour:

> For the doctrine of the Holy Spirit means that we acknowledge and adore the everywhere-present pressure of God; not only as a peculiar religious experience, not as a grace or influence sent out from another world or order, but as a personal holy Presence and Energy, the Lord *(sic)* and Giver of Life -- in this world and yet distinct from it, penetrating all, yet other than all, the decisive factor in every situation. It means God entering into, working on and using the whole world of things, events, and persons; operating at various levels,

and most deeply in that world of souls where His*(sic)* creation shows a certain kinship with Himself.

And this Presence is moulding, helping and pressing all His creation – on every plane, in every person, at every point -- by the direct action of His divine influence, to move towards greater perfection, get nearer the pattern of his shining thought. That influence may be felt as the gentle pressure on which piety prefers to dwell, or as the shattering invasion of a compelling and purifying power. . . . When we meditate on all this, we get a wonderful sense of the unmeasured action of God, and the links that bind together the mysterious rhythms of nature, the great movements of history, and the hidden springs of Providence and prayer.

("The Golden Sequence",12-13)

Underhill sets before us the Indwelling Spirit, "moulding, helping and pressing", patient and open to human need. For those whose faith in God finds its chief anchor in Jesus of Nazareth, the pervasive Sacred Presence is known to be 'foolish' (as perceived by human wisdom) and 'weak' (as perceived by human power). As Christians we have learned to trust the vulnerable divine foolishness and weakness which daily accompany us.. This is the One who carries in sorrowing love our human refusals to live the way of love, the One who gently leads us into the wide paths of truth and beauty.

However, without wishing to diminish this emphasis on the indwelling presence of Spirit in each person, we must stress that this presence is not known first as a gift to individual persons. Before the development of urban living, the Sacred was believed to dwell within the total community formed by humans, animals, the living Earth and the surrounding cosmos. In the biblical tradition, long before Israel came to believe in the possibility of personal relationship with God, Israel knew Yahweh as present to the chosen people in one community of faith. And the same was true for Jesus of Nazareth. He laboured for the coming of the Reign of Righteousness and Truth among his disciples, people called to be a Spirit-filled community within which each person was nurtured in faith.

Unfortunately, this central truth has been obscured by the rampant individualism of the West, by a culture which exalts individual effort and worth and denies the fundamental significance of society and of human social relations. The full context within which the Divine is revealed as Indwelling Presence is always one of persons bound together in community. Personal faith grows by participation in a community of faith.

The gifts of the Indwelling Spirit are not always comforting in the colloquial sense, but they are always comforting in the root sense (Latin: to make strong). Communities and persons who respond with open hearts to the Holy One can expect to receive gifts of the Spirit and to be led into new life. These gifts are unceasing in their splendour and power. They guide us into thanksgiving for the divine generosity, they enable us to repent for personal and social sin, they confer spiritual healing and wisdom, and they help us to become creative and compassionate expressions of the vital divine loving. Gathered into faith communities, we can expect to be led where injustice and oppression must be challenged, and where the power of love must go "to do justice and to love kindness". In the process, we shall find a Way of life which is truly Good News for our time.

CHAPTER SUMMARY

As we enter into the task of developing new images of God, substantial changes in our understanding of worship become inevitable. This will include a thorough-going revision of our language about sin, repentance, forgiveness and atonement. Unfortunately, traditional Christian liturgy obscures the constant and generous presence of the compassionate God. We have used "invocation" as though God were absent and waits to be invited into our assemblies. On the contrary, there is always Sacred Presence waiting to be known, waiting for our faithful response. We must transform our religious assemblies so that we gather as children coming to a loving God who eagerly awaits us. We come in need of healing, teaching, inspiration, courage and renewed community. We come to receive so that we may be enabled to live in the world with gratitude and good works.

Prayer is an event in which we bring ourselves into the Presence - for thanksgiving, forgiveness and healing, and to become aware of tasks to be undertaken for the healing of Earth and all her creatures. Personal prayer is an opportunity to take up our spiritual journey in a regular and disciplined manner, and to reflect upon our moral responsibilities.

Prayer is also a time for complaint, for protest. Much of life brings pain and suffering. There will be times to share with God the suffering which comes from living in a troubled and violent world, and to be strengthened as persons who can bring healing to social and economic life.

We live in a time of transition which is exciting, challenging and rewarding. This is a time of overlap between an 'old time religion' which is in decline, and a vital, new awareness of Sacred Presence in the entire cosmos, which is struggling to be born. An old Story is giving place to the new Story.

Within the cosmos as a whole, and especially in Earth and in all her creatures, we celebrate Sacred Presence, Indwelling Spirit. The Spirit constantly urges us into community with one another, not only because this is natural for us but also because the divine Word can be heard and accepted truthfully only as we share our spiritual quest with sisters and brothers in faith. Our communal walk with the generous God holds an invitation to rediscover the sacredness of the cosmos, in all its parts, and to live with a new and vibrant stewardship.

> Gracious God, You are Sacred Presence hidden from us,
> > but You give yourself to us in overwhelming generosity.
> You break open our hearts with the floodtide of your loving,
> > You inflame our minds with the wonder of your speaking.
> You bind up our soul wounds with your gentle compassion,
> > You gird our wills with the strength of your Spirit.
> You give us pilgrim friends with whom to share the journey.
> > From dawn to dark, in joy and thanksgiving,
> > we celebrate your presence in our lives,
> > our lives in your presence.

APPENDIX A

RELIGIONS OF THE ANCIE
MEDITERRANEAN WORLD

Christianity emerged into a world which was saturated
The new Jesus movement, which sprang up after his deati
assortment of religions which over centuries had found
themselves throughout the Mediterranean region. Our purpose
to describe briefly the most significant practices of these religions
were present within the territory of imperial Rome, and to suggest
one common element in these religions exerted an unfortun
influence on the development of Christianity.

Classical Greek religion emerged late in the second millenium BCE
when illiterate bards composed and sang epic poems extolling the
Olympian gods. With the invention of an alphabetic script in the eighth
century BCE, an important poet, Hesiod, wrote about how the gods were
born and had developed into an inter-related pantheon. A greater poet
whom we know as Homer, gave classic expression to the deeds of these
legendary divinities in his books, the Iliad and the Odyssey. These works
profoundly influenced every aspect of the life in the Greek city states of
the 6th to 4th centuries. In the city states

> . . . there were places and times that were especially
> sacred and set apart exclusively for sacred uses, but
> there were no great secular spaces from which thought
> of the gods was excluded as inappropriate. The
> presence of the gods was everywhere and at all times
> evoked by shrines and rituals . . . . Most of the finest
> public buildings were temples, and all civic festivals were
> religious festivals.
>
> > ("The Ancient and Continuing Pieties of the
> > Greek World in Classical Mediterranean Spirituality",
> > A.H. Armstrong, ed., 68)

> The gods were apprehended and worshipped as far
> more powerful than human beings. They were not
> omnipotent and they did not stand free from the universe
> and act upon it from the outside. They were powers in
> the world and were limited by the powers of other gods

and the law of the whole. . . . This great power of the gods in the nature of things was an everlasting power. They were immortal.

(ibid, 74)

In the fifth and fourth centuries the famous classical teachers Socrates, Plato and Aristotle occupied commanding intellectual heights of Greek society. Several important but less influential philosophers taught before and after them, but these three offered a major critique of the outrageous and immoral behaviour of the gods and so moved Greek religion towards more rational and less mythological expression. In contrast to the traditional and popular mythical pantheon, they offered metaphysical insights informed by rational thought. The entire cluster of respected classical Greek teachers was responsible for developing an erudite tradition of philosophy, politics and religion. This intellectual legacy, together with Greek art, architecture and civic practice, gave form and substance to the continuing influence of classical Greece up to present times.

A different religious culture emerged on the Italian peninsula, perhaps as early as the fifth century BCE. For the early Etruscans and later Romans, 'piety' acquired a local and practical connotation:

> . . . the proper and correct performance of due rituals was an important part of Roman piety, of Roman spirituality. But the word [piety] goes further than that and implies the recognition and performance of all due obligations - moral and emotional as well as ritual - to family, friends, country, and indeed to anybody with whom one comes in contact.

(J. Pinsent, "Roman Spirituality",
in Armstrong, op,cit., 168)

When compared with the Greek gods, the Roman pantheon had a more down-to-earth and less poetic cast:

> "Fallow-plower, Renewer, Ridge-plower, Grafter, Plower-up, Harrower, Hoer, Weeder, Reaper, Gatherer, Storer, Bringer-forth. . . . [These names] attest the very real Roman feeling that every activity of life was under the influence of a divine power".

(ibid, 178-9)

Pinsent comments: "The developed Homeric and Hesiodic pantheon was never, for the Romans, much more than a poetic device." Rome, during its life as a republic, was robustly pragmatic.

The famed republic, however, fell upon difficult times during many years of civil war. When the internal conflict finally ended in 31 BCE, the people were morally and spiritually depleted - and the republic became the empire. The victorious general Octavius, who had taken the title Caesar Augustus, encouraged and supported a religious revival. Unfortunately, the revival did not outlast his death since traditional religion had become unable to offer adequate spiritual resources to the people of the Italian peninsula. This opened the door to non-Roman universalist cults from other nations, one of which came from Egypt.

A very different expression of religious devotion had emerged in Egypt long before the age of classical Greece and Rome. Existing monuments of the third millenium BCE give evidence that the pharaohs believed that in death they would experience union with the god Osiris and companionship with the sun-god, Re. Later we find mention of the major gods Horus and Seth amidst a multitude of other deities. Osiris, god of the dead, was for centuries the most popular god, "although he was eclipsed during the Graeco-Roman period by his sister and wife Isis" (J.G. Griffiths, "The Faith of the Pharaonic Period", in Armstrong, *op.cit.*, 5).

As a result of a sequence of imperial invasions of Egypt by Babylon, Persia, Greece and Rome, and the consequent establishing of networks of trade, devotion to Isis became extended far beyond northeastern Africa. An influential salvation cult associated with the goddess began to be practised in major centres of the entire Mediterranean region. A native of Madauros in Roman North Africa, Apuleius, gives an extensive account of the cult in his literary work Metamorphoses, where the central figure is Lucius:

> Lucius begs the high priest for admission into "the secret rites of the holy night." The priest [of Isis] administers suitable warnings, stressing that "the gates of hell and the guarantees of life were alike in the power of the goddess, and the rite of dedication itself was performed in the manner of a voluntary death and of a life obtained

by grace" . . . . the old life will end and a new life will begin, for the goddess by her providence caused the initiate "in some way to be born again."

(J. G. Griffiths,
"The Great Egyptian Cults of Oecumenical Significance",
in Armstrong, *op.cit.*, 55)

A fourth religion which also spread widely because of imperial conquests and patterns of trade was that of Mithras. Originally this religion was associated with the Persian sage Zoroaster, confined to men, and favoured by soldiers and merchants. One of its secret rites involved speaking the sounds of the seven vowels of the alphabet "with 'elemental' force ('with fire and spirit') to reveal the seven planetary Gods and their realms" ("In Praise of Nonsense", P.C. Miller, in Armstrong, *op.cit.*, 498). The prescribed, mystical use of select letters of the alphabet and of certain numbers was believed to have special significance, a practice also found in other religious societies. Mithraism was the only one of the known universalist cults which did not have a public expression; the devotees met in private gatherings.

A universal type of religious practice widely adopted throughout the ancient Mediterranean world was 'the mysteries'. Each of the classical Greek, Roman, Egyptian and Persian religions, and eventually Christianity, lent itself to some variant of this form.

> The term 'mysteries' seems to have attached itself first to an ancient celebration at Eleusis, near Athens, and was associated with the goddess Demeter. . . . [Mysteries] were a survival of the archaic experience of ritual time. More characteristic and compelling still was the sense of security they induced concerning one's personal good fortune in the world to come. . . . Later, other mysteries from the East joined the Eleusian in providing this experience. Those of Egyptian Isis or Persian Mithras or the Syrian Great Mother were popular in Roman times. The mysteries of Jesus Christ, baptism and eucharist, were not untouched by this sensibility as they spread through the Graeco-Roman world. . . . the mysteries accomplished an awakening and showing of the divine within the self.

(P. Manchester,
"The Religious Experience of Time and Eternity",
in Armstrong, *op.cit.*, 392)

Thus these several ancient Mediterranean religions found expression in a plentitude of forms and a multitude of associations, both public and private. But one more religion needs to be mentioned here.

Scattered throughout much of the Mediterranean region was the faith and practice of Judaism. From their homeland of ancient Israel, Jews of the diaspora had taken with them an observance of the sacred Torah which included the founding of synagogues in many important urban centres. And, as Alan Segal demonstrates in "Paul the Convert", some Jews also held to an apocalyptic mysticism: transformation of the faithful into God at the Close of the Age.

For the new Jesus movement Jewish mysticism was of great significance, since in its beginnings the movement was a sect of Judaism and it expected to find there a source of converts. Alan Segal proposes that Jewish mysticism contributed significantly to the development of early Christian doctrine, especially in Paul's mystical teaching that baptized Christians live *en Christo*, "in Christ". The Eastern Orthodox Church has emphasized the theme of divinization of the Christian in the Christ as the telos, the fulfilment, of the Christian life. Christianity under Roman influence, however, has hardly noticed this teaching and instead made much of Paul's revision of the meaning of the Law.

This brief overview reveals the central place which religion occupied in the ancient Mediterranean world. It is not an overstatement to describe that world as "saturated with religion". It is a picture of intense preoccupation with the life of 'spirit'. In contrast, the 'flesh' is downgraded, despised, or utterly rejected, depending on the degree of otherworldliness being encouraged. The Encyclopedia Britannica, in the article "Hellenistic Religion", comments:

> Most Hellenistic religions offered a highly dualistic
> cosmology in which the earthly realm in all its aspects . . .
> constituted the imprisoning power of evil over the soul.
> Liberation was attainable through cultic activity, secret
> knowledge (gnosis), and divine intervention.

A highly intellectualized form of this dualistic religion was present in the teaching of the famed Jewish Neoplatonist philosopher, Plotinus, which greatly influenced the development of early Christian thought.

Concerning his teachings, P. Hadot comments:

> First, they describe the journey by which the soul can try
> to ascend toward the divine, so that the experience of
> union may be possible. In ascending through the
> hierarchical levels of reality, the soul passed through the
> stages of spiritual progress; that is to say, it brought
> about a radical transformation of the whole being.
> ("Neoplatonic Spirituality", in Armstrong, *op.cit.*, 234)

These comments apply specifically to the religious preoccupations of
the wealthy and sophisticated minority of people. Religion had a
somewhat different aspect among the peasants. H. D. Saffrey refers to

> . . . peasants' festivities, in the shadow of the temple -
> pauses in an exhausting life, moments of rest from
> unending labour. As long as they could celebrate the
> feast with a sacrifice offered to the gods, they did so;
> afterwards, they confined themselves to an offering of
> incense and to a private family feast accompanied by
> songs and prayers.
>
> ("The Piety and Prayers of
> Ordinary Men and Women in Late Antiquity",
> in Armstrong, *op.cit.*, 201)

However, there is no reason to believe that these rural folk were less
subject than the intelligensia to the otherworldly teachings of religion.
They simply did not have the time, leisure nor financial means to engage
in intensive spiritual disciplines or esoteric societies.

Classical Mediterranean religion, then, was everywhere concerned
with providing an escape from the material order, to provide a release
from bondage to the flesh. In this way any person could rise to the divine
realms and be united to Ultimate Reality. Myths of an evil material order
and of deliverance by divine grace were present in all religions of that
time. It is vitally important then, for the purposes of this book, to notice
how central this particular viewpoint was in the general religious ethos of
the time. This was the dominating religious climate within which the
Christian church emerged.

Within the new Jesus movement in Roman Palestine, household
groups remained rooted in the words and works of Jesus concerning the

Reign of God on earth (as evident especially in the Synoptic gospels and in the Didache). But very soon, in the latter decades of the first century, other Christians were beginning to refashion their faith as one more myth of eternal salvation. By the time Athanasius became Bishop of Alexandria (328), he was able to write a sophisticated apologia for the Christian myth of salvation. We can trace the heart of his argument in selections from Sections 5 to 8 in his "Treatise on the Incarnation of the Word of God":

> This, then, was the plight of men (*sic*). God had not only made them out of nothing, but had also graciously bestowed on them His own life by the grace of the Word. Then, turning from eternal things to things corruptible, by counsel of the devil, they had become the cause of their own corruption in death . . . .
> . . . because death and corruption were gaining ever firmer hold on them, the human race was in process of destruction. . . . The law of death, which followed from the Transgression [Adam's sin], prevailed upon us, and from it was no escape.
> . . . Had it been a case of a trespass only, and not of subsequent corruption, repentance would have been well enough; but when once the transgression had begun, men came under the power of corruption proper to their nature and were bereft of the grace which belonged to the Image of God. . . . Who was it that was needed for such grace and such recall as we required? Who, save the Word of God Himself.
> . . . It was by surrendering to death the body which He [Jesus] had taken, as an offering and sacrifice free from every stain, that He forthwith abolished death for his human brethren by the offering of the equivalent.

In this Treatise we are a great distance from the words and works of Jesus of Nazareth which announced the breaking into history of the Reign of God. Instead, we are securely within the realm of a Christian myth of salvation which accents a particular interpretation of Jesus' death and resurrection. The search for eternal life, which was so universally evident in all other religions, became rooted also in the new religion of Jesus the Christ. Was this simply an accident of doctrinal synchronicity? Or is this evidence of a subtle and yet irresistible ideological pressure on the early church to turn its attention away from Jesus' commitment to the transformation of personal and social life in this world, and toward a

159

religious practice primarily concerned with eternal life? The latter seems to be the better explanation.

This fundamental shift in emphasis within the early church provided the spiritual foundation for the church of the ages. Concern for personal salvation subsequently dominated the faith of the majority of Christians; only a minority remained committed to the tasks of personal transformation and of leading society towards a public practice of compassion and justice as central to Jesus' Way.

APPENDIX B

LITURGICAL SAMPLE

Community Thanksgiving:

Leader: Let us remember all those women who face an unknown future
with faith and courage.

We give thanks for:

all women who challenge social norms and traditions and dare to stand
up;

all women facing hardships in life but who never give up;

all women being abused by their spouses and yet brave enough to find a
way out for themselves;

all women single parents who are strong enough to shoulder the
responsibility of raising their children;

all women who are discriminated against for their sexual inclination but
who can still affirm themselves;

all women who are under threat of unemployment, insufficient work, or
change of employment but still do not give up;

all women pastors and workers who work wholeheartedly to keep the
church faithful;

All: O God, we thank you.

Naming our Weeping:

L: Where is the pain in our lives?
(gathered in a large circle, the women briefly share the source of their
pain)

After each sharing, L: You are not alone. All: Your tears are our tears.

Affirming our strength:

L: Who are the women who have given us strength and courage, the
creative models for our lives? (names are called out by the women)

L: These women walk with us.

All: We are not alone.

Commitment to each other:

L: In the face of all our realities

All: We are the people who heal each other, who grow strong together, who name the truth, who know what it means to live in community, who survive well.

Interecessory prayer:

Response: We so pray, God; grant us courage to do something about it. Amen.

L: Let us pray for the women in our community who just gave birth, but have no means to support their babies and families.

All: Response

L: Let us pray for the women and men who have migrated to cities and abroad due to unemployment here.

All: Response

L: Let us pray for the women who are physically and sexually abused in the home and outside the home.

All: Response

L: Let us pray for the street children and the homeless, for those whose bodies and future seem destroyed by illegal drugs, family break-down, and poverty.

All: Response

L: Let us pray for our indigenous sisters and brothers and for their struggle for land and culture.

All: Response

L: Let us pray that the trees, animals, rivers and seas be spared from further destruction and exploitation.

All: Response

L: Let pray for and remember the people suffering due to volcanic eruptions and natural calamities.

All: Response

BIBLIOGRAPHY

Anonymous. 1978.   The Cloud of Unknowing, tr. I. Progoff.
                                                    Dell Publishing.
Anonymous. 1952.   The Way of a Pilgrim, tr. R.M. French.
                                                    Harper & Bros.
Asian Women's Resource Centre. In God's Image.
                                           Kuala Lumpur, Malaysia.
Berry, Thomas. 1998.   The Dream of the Earth.
                                      Sierra Club Books, San Francisco.
Bonhoeffer, Dietrich. 1964.   The Cost of Discipleship. SCM Press.

_____ 1964.   Letters and Papers from Prison.
                                           Collins (Fontana Books).
Bloom, Harold. 1991.   The Book of J. Random House. Vintage Books.

Borg, Marcus. 1995.   Meeting Jesus Again for the First Time.
                                                    HarperCollins.
Brueggemann, Walter. 1992.   Old Testament Theology. Fortress Press.

Chesterton, G.K. 1960.   St. Francis of Assisi. Hodder & Stoughton.

Crossan, J.D. 2001.   Excavating Jesus. HarperSanFrancisco.

Eliade, Mircea. 1957.   The Sacred and The Profane.
                                      Harcourt, Brace & World, Inc.
Fenton, J.C. 1971.   Saint Matthew. Penguin Books.

Finkelstein, I. and Silberman, N.   2001.   The Bible Unearthed.
                                      Simon & Shuster. Touchstone Book.
Fletcher, Richard. 1997.   The Barbarian Conversion. Henry Holt & Co.

Friedman, Richard E. 1998.   The Hidden Book in the Bible.
                                                    HarperSanFrancisco.

Funk, Robert W. 1996. Honest to Jesus. HarperSanFrancisco.

Goodenough, Ursula. 1998. The Sacred Depths of Nature.
                                    Oxford University Press.
Gutierrez, Gustavo. 1984. We Drink from our own Wells. Orbis Books.

Herzog, William R. 1994. Parables as Subversive Speech.
                                    Westminster.
Hirsch, Edward. 1999. How To Read a Poem.
                                    Harcourt, A Harvest Book.
Horsley, Richard A. 2003. Jesus and Empire. Fortress Press.

Horsley, R. and Silberman N. 1997. The Message and the Kingdom.
                                    Grosset/Putnam.
James, William. 1923. The Varieties of Religious Experience.
                                    Longman, Green & Co.
Johnson, Elizabeth A. 1992. She Who Is. Crossroads.

Julian of Norwich. 1978. Showings. Paulist Press.

Kazantzakis, Nikos. 1965. Report to Greco. Simon & Schuster.

Kelly, Thomas. 1941. A Testament of Devotion. Harper & Bros.

Lonergan, Bernard. 1972. Method in Theology. Herder and Herder.

Malone, Mary T. 2000. Women and Christianity: Vol. 1. Novalis

_____ 2001. Women and Christianity: Vol. 2. Novalis/Orbis.

_____ 2003. Women and Christianity: Vol. 3. Novalis/Orbis

Morgan, John S. 1974. When the Morning Stars Sang Together.
                                    Book Society of Canada.
Murphy, F.J. 1991. The Religious World of Jesus. Abingdon Press.

Myers, Chad. 1988. Binding the Strong Man. Orbis Books.

Quinlan, Will. 1951. The Temple of God's Wounds.
Morehouse-Gorham.
Religious Society of Friends, Britain. 1995. Advices and Queries.
Warwick Printing.
Richardson, Alan, ed. 1957. A Theological Word Book of the Bible.
SCM Press.
Ross, Rupert. 1996. Returning to the Teachings. Penguin Books.

Rowland, Wade. 1999. Ockham's Razor. Key Porter Books.

Schussler Fiorenza, Elisabeth. 1984. In Memory of Her. Crossroads.

Segal, Alan F. 1990. Paul the Convert. Yale University Press.

Swimme, Brian. 1996. The Hidden Heart of the Cosmos. Orbis Books.

Swimme, B. and Berry, T. 1992. The Universe Story.
HarperSanFrancisco.
Teilhard de Chardin, P. 1959. The Phenomenon of Man.
Harper Collins.
Temple, William. 1961. Readings in St. John's Gospel. Macmillan & Co.

Theissen, Gerd. 1992. Social Reality and the Early Christians.
Fortress Press.
Third World Theologians. 1989.
The Road to Damascus: Kairos to Conversion
Centre of Concern, Wa., D.C.
Thompson, T.L. 1999. The Bible in History. Jonathon Cape.

Tillich, Paul. 1957. Dynamics of Faith. Harper Colophon Books.

_____ 1975. The Courage To Be. Yale University Press.

Toolan, David. 2001. At Home in the Cosmos. Orbis Press.

de Tourville, Abbé. 1982. Letters of Direction (L. Menzies, ed.).
                                        Mowbray.

Underhill, Evelyn. 1914. Practical Mysticism for Normal People.
                                        J.M. Dent & Sons.

_____ 1933. The Golden Sequence. Harper Torchbook.

_____ 2002. Mysticism. Dover Publications. (1st Ed. 1911)

Ward, Benedicta. 1975. The Wisdom of the Desert Fathers.
                                        SLG Press, Oxford.

Ward, Keith. 1991. A Vision to Pursue. SCM Press.

Weil, Simone. 1959. Waiting on God. Collins, Fontana Books.

Wilson, A.N. 1997. Paul: The Mind of the Apostle. W.W. Norton & Co.

Wink, Walter. 1992. Engaging the Powers. Fortress Press.